"Angelina, no . . .

David said, emotionally ravaged. He ___ tearstained face in his hands. "I would never leave you. Never."

"Oh, David," Angelina choked, "you don't know that. If you found out anything about me—"

"I know you! Inside. Outside. Your mind, your heart, your body, Angelina. What more is there to know? And I love you, all of you, and will forever."

Angelina closed her eyes and in despair burrowed against David's chest and sobbed. Now she knew she could not tell him. Over the weekend her fear of being rejected had made her brave, but her love— this maddening love!—rendered her weak. The lie would continue. And whatever time she had with him she would cherish.

Dear Reader,

This month in FOR NOW, FOREVER, the ever-popular Nora Roberts brings to a poignant conclusion her saga of the irrepressible MacGregor clan.

You may remember that the saga started with PLAYING THE ODDS in August 1985, and also included TEMPTING FATE, ALL THE POSSIBILITIES and ONE MAN'S ART. With the publication of FOR NOW, FOREVER, we are reissuing the entire series in a special Collectors Edition. Look for them, with their tartan covers, at your local booksellers, along with this month's Special Editions.

FOR NOW, FOREVER goes back in time to tell how Daniel MacGregor, founder of the MacGregor dynasty, first wooed and won unflappable Anna Whitfield. Whether standing alone or read with the other four, Daniel's and Anna's story will capture your heart, for theirs is undeniably the love of a lifetime!

We hope that you will enjoy this Special Edition today, and will enjoy many more.

Please write to us:

Jane Nicholls
Silhouette Books
PO Box 236
Thornton Road
Croydon
Surrey
CR9 3RU

JENNIFER WEST
Object of Desire

Silhouette Special Edition

Originally Published by Silhouette Books
a division of
Harlequin Enterprises Ltd.

First published in Great Britain in 1987
by Silhouette Books, 15–16 Brook's Mews, London W1A 1DR

© Jennifer West 1987

Silhouette, Silhouette Special Edition and Colophon are
Trade Marks of Harlequin Enterprises B.V.

ISBN 0 373 50620 1

23–0687

Printed and bound in Great Britain by
Cox & Wyman Ltd, Reading

To Ram Butler . . . whose words make
real miracles happen every moment . . . my
thanks and love.

JENNIFER WEST's

current hobby is tracing her roots to see if she has a
claim to any European throne. In the meantime, she
writes novels, television scripts and short stories.
Jennifer's husband, son, two Akita dogs and an in-
determinate number of goldfish put up with her at
their residence in Irvine, California.

Other Silhouette Books by Jennifer West

Silhouette Special Edition

Earth and Fire
Return to Paradise

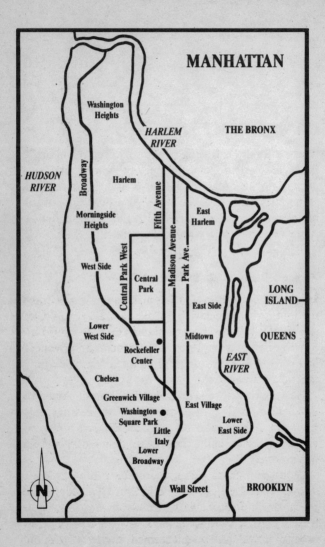

Chapter One

Guido Rufio was more than picky as to who worked for him in his Greenwich Village delicatessen; Guido was paranoid. How many times had he been ripped off by customers and employees alike in the twenty years he had been in business? Enough to make him semicrazy, that's how many times.

He was therefore skeptical when he put Angelina Zarsuela on Deli Italia's payroll. Who was she anyway? His daughter's friend, that's all; just a girl enrolled in the same ballet class. Other than that, Angelina was no one.

Guido only hired people whose genealogy he knew through the old neighborhood in Brooklyn. But he had pretty much shaken all the family trees of available fruit. The kids were students of law these days. They went to "clerk"; no one, it seemed, wanted to dish out pickles and slice prosciutto anymore.

And so it was that Guido Rufio came to hire Angelina Zarsuela, a someone who was no one.

That was three years ago, and in that time Guido had come to accept with reservation—distrust ran in his blood where white blood cells flowed in the veins of others—that Angelina Zarsuela was as scrupulously honest as she was efficient.

As it turned out, she was also possessed of another attribute that made her Guido's most valued employee. The delicate, dark-haired beauty had a strange talent that saved him thousands of dollars each year. Angelina, Guido discovered, had eyes in the back of her head.

Angelina had the second sight for anticipating who was going to rip off a salami or a container of butter—almost, Guido secretly thought, before the thief, himself, knew.

Such a situation occurred on the morning of October 14. The scene was such: it was shortly before noon and Angelina was helping a blind man locate the items on his shopping list. Guido was restocking the refrigerator section in the back of the store. He had one eye on the cash register in the front, while he spoke to a tall, good-looking man who was asking him if, as a first generation immigrant, he felt America had lived up to its promise of being the land of opportunity and freedom.

He was weighing his response to the question when a sudden ruckus erupted in another part of the store.

Guido arrived at the front door just after Angelina. She had hold of the blind man's jacket and was whirling him around by the back hemline.

It all happened so quickly that Guido was breathless just from watching.

Angelina made a lightning-quick feint for the man's right side, and as he went to defend himself she grabbed beneath the jacket's left arm and tore away a net bag containing various expensive delicacies stocked by Guido for his more discerning clients.

"My smoked Danish sausages!" Guido wailed as the can whizzed past him on its side. "And the snails! My beautiful escargot! You devil!" A glance at the man's booty told Guido he would have easily been taken for a hundred dollars.

The man—who was anything but blind—made a crafty lunge toward a fallen can of caviar. Angelina kicked him. The man yelped and limped backward, then screamed a profanity at Angelina.

In turn, Angelina responded with something sounding equally vehement in a tongue that Guido could not quite place. Melodious, strident, comforting, and terrifying: it held all of these qualities at the same time. It was a language fallen into the cracks of Spanish, French and Slavic. The sounds raced after the thief as he bolted for freedom.

Angelina bent immediately to her knees and began to retrieve the fallen cans. "Show his face around here again, *he'll* be a sausage," she muttered under her breath. "Make that goose liver pâté," she reconsidered ominously as she picked up a can of the same.

Guido rarely felt chivalrous or behaved in any way courtly. This was one time. Gallantly, he lifted her up by the elbow. "Angelina, Angelina…my little one…are you all right?"

"I'd feel better if I could have flattened him."

"He seemed to be limping," Guido advised consolingly.

"Hobbled right out of here! Great kick, best damn kick I've ever seen." The voice came out of nowhere.

Both Angelina and Guido turned, locating the speaker. It was the man Guido had been talking with prior to the incident. He had edged in closer to the nearby bread section.

Angelina stared, vaguely considering the man. She wasn't sure about him. She wasn't certain if he was making fun of her or if the smile he wore was genuinely admiring. So she ignored him.

Guido did not. "She has an extraordinary extension," he bragged. He recalled his daughter saying this about Angelina's ability to leap higher and farther and longer than anyone in their class. His daughter had often said that Angelina was extraordinary. Guido did not know about her artistic merit; he only knew about Parma ham and good pasta. But now, here in his own deli, even he had proof. "This young woman is most extraordinary," he said proudly, beaming a smile at Angelina.

The man tilted his head and nodded. "That's pretty obvious."

The way he said it made Angelina blush. The three words were low and slow and, well, it was ridiculous that three words could say nothing and yet say so much. She could feel her face growing warm under his green gaze. A flood of heat seeped through her body.

"Now, you—out!" Guido barked, back to his old self. "Freedom is yours. Go . . . leave early."

Rescued, Angelina looked away from the customer to Guido. "With pay, or without?" she challenged.

"What? You want pay, too?" Guido threw up his hands in mock despair. "Of course, pay. You think I am some cheap son of a gun or something?"

"Yes," Angelina said. "You can add petty tyrant, too."

"I am," he agreed. "But not today. Go..." Guido insisted again, shooing her along. He smiled. It made him glad to see the young woman's face so alight with beauty. He loved his daughter and she was pretty, but in his heart Guido knew that Angelina was special, very special, and not only for her beauty; there was a quality, a *something* about her. In a starlit sky, Angelina Zarsuela would shine out brighter than all.

Angelina kissed Guido on the cheek. "You're really not half so bad. I love you," she said.

"Yes," Guido grunted, pleased and embarrassed because he found himself overwhelmed by the tenderness of feeling between them. "Obviously, you should. I am a wonderful man—half of me is." Angelina laughed. "So put on your pink dancing shoes and practice. Practice, practice!" He waved his hands in the air and went off behind the counter. "One day I will bring my entire family to the ballet where Angelina Zarsuela will be prima ballerina. Perhaps someone will make a great ballet for you to dance...a story about the love of a pickle for a salami! Very dramatic. Maybe I will do it myself. I am wonderful and I am talented."

"You are crazy, Guido Rufio!" She turned, laughing and crashed full-on against the man with the disconcerting green eyes.

He had come up behind her on his way to pay. He held one of the small red plastic shopping baskets, half-filled with canned goods and odds and ends. In a glance—one of her potent see-all sweeps—Angelina noted that the sizes and amounts of his goods were small. Conclusion: he was single. He liked expensive things. He liked unusual things. It made no difference to her, these cursory observations; it was merely part of her nature to note everything.

"Sorry," she said curtly, pulling back from him and trying to avoid the green grip of his eyes.

"Excuse *me*," he returned, and stepped to the side just when she did. They moved again. Both stopped.

"Which way are you going?" she asked flatly.

"I don't know," he answered back just as matter-of-factly. "Which way do you think I should go?"

"I'm going to take a step to the right."

"Will that be your right, or mine?"

Angelina let out a sigh of exasperation. "My right."

"Very good. Then that would apparently make it my left. It's always wise to have a plan before setting out, don't you think?"

She stared at him. He stared back, undaunted by her obvious coldness. "Very amusing," she said.

"Perhaps silly. This *is* silly."

"You're saying I'm silly? I'm silly because I am trying to get out of here before the spring thaw?"

"Not you particularly—although I don't know you well enough to say. I was thinking in terms of the situation. The situation is silly. You, on the other hand, are argumentative."

"And you're arrogant."

"I don't mean to be," he said agreeably. The emerald eyes laughed. "I'm just genuinely impressed by your valor. And, since you don't seem to be the type of woman who is prone to bubble over with friendliness in a chance social encounter, well, I figured the best way to engage you in conversation is to have a direct confrontation." He smiled amiably. "You seem to like direct confrontations."

"You're so terribly clever. You've got everything figured out, don't you? Except which way to step and how to end a perfectly ridiculous and pointless conversation." She said it sarcastically, but, in fact, there was something ingenious about him—which was the underlying reason she was still standing there bantering. Your usual kind of guy would have long since backed down in the face of her obvious disinterest. So she had to give him points for persistence. Most men were intimidated by her frostiness. In fact, she considered her ability to ice people one of the best of her "bad" talents.

Vaguely, without particular interest, she noted the man was tall and blond and extremely attractive. Superficially, anyway. There was even a slight cleft in his chin. He reminded her of the men who posed for sportswear in the expensive magazines. The arms of a sweater were knotted around his neck. She could imagine him on the deck of a yacht. Fair of hair, he appeared glossy as a page, himself, as if nature had shined him to a smoothly perfect finish. And the finish was a golden brown.

Tanned! Could one believe it? In New York City, in what was becoming winter, the man had the nerve to flaunt summer's glow.

The clothes he wore were conservative and on his lean frame the brown corduroy pants and blue button-down shirt took on a casually expensive élan. On someone else the outfit might have appeared stodgy. But something in his manner gave the clothes a personality. It was his attitude, a kind of built-in arrogance born of class privilege. Angelina knew it well, but only from observation. She, herself, had been spawned on the opposite end of the social spectrum.

All of this ran through Angelina's mind automatically, with no more effort than it took to breathe. The facility of character assessment was the result of childhood training. She had learned early to gauge a person's position in life by subtleties overlooked by those whose survival did not depend upon such accurate analysis.

"You'd be great in the ring," the man said.

"Not enough competition. I prefer the streets." That was it, she'd had enough. Any more conversation and he'd start to get ideas, wrong ideas. To her, life was an enormous animate museum through which she strolled and picked up information useful to accomplishing her aims. In this case, she had merely browsed a minute or two longer than she had intended. But he wouldn't know that. He'd think he was moving in on her. And with that, she started to move away.

He reached out quickly, holding her back. Angelina gave him a dark look. He smiled slightly and let go of her arm. "Look, all kidding aside, that guy could have done some serious damage. You were lucky. This time," he added.

"I'm touched, really moved by the concern. But don't lose any sleep over it. See these feet? They know how to run when they have to."

"Have they ever had to?"

For an answer, Angelina gave him a piercing drop-dead look. Anyone else would have withered away on the spot. But the look didn't faze him. He was smiling again, seeming to enjoy something about their meeting that entirely eluded her.

"Most people don't take risks," the stranger explained. "Not anymore. So you're unusual. A phenomenon in your own time."

The speech made Angelina uncomfortable, summoning as it did old memories from the past better left buried. The truth was, she hadn't thought anything about going after the shoplifter. There was no particular bravery involved. She had merely responded automatically. The instinct to react immediately to protect one's property had been drilled into her from early childhood.

"Good," she said. "A phenomenon's a start. So happens I'm shooting for legend. Look, don't mean to break things up, but I've got a destiny to fulfill, see. And I'd kinda like to do it in this lifetime."

This time he let her go.

All he said after her was, "Hey! I'm serious... watch yourself. You might have been killed."

"So might the other guy!" Angelina shot back over her shoulder. Fear of other people wasn't high on her list of concerns. She marched to the back of the store to collect her things, her thoughts already out the door and traveling up West Broadway to her ballet class.

David Jordan Winthrop stood where he was, rooted in indecision. He felt a desperate impulse to go after her. He felt the urge to surround her with himself. It was overwhelmingly strange, and strangely overwhelming, this effect the woman had on him. God, he really had behaved badly! Like some schoolboy pickup, probably; some callow, goony youth hot to trot. That's undoubtedly how his little performance must have come across.

Helpless! He had been momentarily helpless in her presence. Mesmerized. Hypnotized. And now ostracized!

He deserved it, he supposed.

He had needed to keep her engaged in conversation, as if the words were threads tying her to him. Yet, even as he thought it, the spool was unraveling, the distance between them increasing. She wasn't even listening to his warning; that much was clear. The rest of her was a mystery.

He stood there by the frozen food section, paralyzed in his fascination with a young woman of whom he had no knowledge, no social connection, no nothing. Yet, hooked he was, like the frozen fish staring up at him in their beds of cellophane.

All he could do was to continue to follow her with his eyes. How unusual she was; one could feel her distinctiveness just being in her presence. There was a certainty, a focus to her. This woman was...well, he didn't know. She was *something*. A legend about to happen? David shook his head. No rocks fell out. That was something, at least. Now he understood how Alice had felt, falling down the rabbit hole. Things were strange in the pit of his mind; odd feelings, events defying ordinary experience made to seem usual, inside-out conversation.

A new customer had entered the store. The man wore a long African robe with a leather motorcycle jacket over it and a helmet. David shrugged. Of course. Who else? It had to be the Mad Hatter. That's the way things were currently going...

When she came by again, out from the back, David was at the counter, paying Guido for his groceries. The Mad Hatter was at his side with two six-packs of beer. He was enormous and his hands were completely tattooed with roses and hearts and a single worm peeking out from a leaf.

David stared down at the worm, which was smiling.

"It's a social statement," the man said to David.

"Yes. I can see that. And a very powerful one at that."

At Angelina's reappearance, David's senses changed frequency, foregoing the worm and tuning in to the woman. A band of singing elephants might have flown past. Little would he have cared.

For the time being, she—this scrappy warrior woman—was the sole object of his interest; the sole channel coming into his receiver. At the moment she was jamming all other stations.

He watched her covertly as she made her way through the store. Her slender frame was encased in an oversized jacket. A paradox: in contrast to her inner dynamism, her appearance brought to mind a fragile femininity of some other day in history. The face was that of a beautiful, porcelain doll, innocent and refined, bearing an inner wisdom beyond the self-contained facade. He noted she was reasonably tall, with a willowy grace not only to her form, but flowing through her movements, as well. Her slightest motion seemed a part of a dance.

But, of course. She was a ballerina, or at least she harbored dreams in that direction. There had been the exchange to that effect between the store's owner and Angelina. *Angelina.* The store's proprietor had called her that. And David had learned earlier, during his aborted interview, that the man's name was Guido Rufio.

Angelina the fledgling legend. It had the ring of a children's book.

David eyed her. She looked too small, too vulnerable to be a legend.

He had known a few of their kind in his day, known his share of "legends" personally, and none of them had come in a package remotely like Angelina's. Besides, the life of a legend was not all it was cracked up to be. His family was testimony to that. Maybe he should tell her to forget the legend bit; better she should stick to pickles and beating up on men three times her size. Overall it might make for a healthier existence.

As she passed by, her smile and her brief words were for Guido.

Ridiculously, David felt himself burning to be included in the scope of her interest. He hunted through his pocket for the right change to complete his purchase. The fumbling was solely to buy time with her. Naturally he was not being obvious. She could hardly suspect; but when he looked up, it was directly into her eyes. That was a mistake.

Their searing darkness penetrated the careful wall of reserve he had built and scrupulously maintained around himself for twenty-eight years. Up to that moment, but for a few minor cracks, the structure had survived intact. Another look like that and he'd be rubble.

Well, he didn't care. Rather, the intrusion of the glance exhilarated him. It enflamed him. The unexpected trespass into his soul lasted less than a second.

And then Angelina was gone.

Unable to move for a moment, David stood where he was, holding silver coins in a palm grown moist.

"Hey, buddy! You gonna do your thing, or what?"

"Yes. Right now, as a matter of fact," David assured the man beside him.

"Good deal."

David put the coins on the counter. Something in him was altered, he could feel the change, as if he had been a house she had entered, moved through, and finally left, carrying with her a treasure. His pulse was mildly uneven, stirred by the excitement of her visit.

Ah, but what he wouldn't give to have equal access to the secret corridors behind the shining dark eyes, to know the thought behind the slight, amused smile.

He felt driven to know about her.

Only he couldn't. There was simply no road to take to get to his destination. At the beginning of the proposed journey, it appeared he was already at a dead end.

Guido rang up the cash transaction. The bells momentarily brought David back. He noticed the Mad Hatter was staring at him.

"Hey," the man whispered from the side of his mouth, "what're you on, anyway? Gotta be some heavy stuff. You look really spaced, man."

David nodded. "Some heavy, heavy stuff."

"Yeah? Bad stuff, huh?"

"Bad."

"Like?" The man waited, seeming as impressed as he was interested.

"Infatuation, I think they call it."

The man thought for a moment, shook his head. "Hey—never heard of it, man."

"Well, you gotta know the right people," David said. "Ask around. It's everywhere. On the streets, in restaurants, beaches, parks . . . everywhere."

Guido was putting his stuff in a bag and the Mad Hatter decided to drift back into the deli for some additional beer while he waited.

David's mind drifted, too. All he had at his disposal was the sport of speculation. It was impossible to judge her nationality by appearance. Of course, by accent, she was clearly American; but there were some other, subtle, international hints to her mannerisms. And what about that foreign language? Strange sounding. He couldn't place it, although he'd been all over the world more times than he could count.

He returned to her appearance. Her skin was a flawless ivory tone, against which the dark radiance of large, almond-shaped eyes shone. Reaching midway down her back, her hair was drawn into a silken black tail that undulated to and fro as she moved.

It had been this sight that had last captivated David as Angelina had moved from the delicatessen into the New York City streets.

Had he gone after her, what might have happened?

Guido handed him his bag, and David fought down the impulse to ask about Angelina. The man wasn't likely to give out any information. This was New York City.

"Thanks," David said and started out. Then he turned and said casually, "I just live down around the corner, so I'll probably be back in now and then. What about if we continue our conversation?"

"What conversation?" Guido asked as he studied a tape from the cash register.

"On American immigrants."

"Sure, sure. It's no big hardship. And it's no big thrill, either. You want to know what I think? I'll tell you. Anything you want to know, I'll tell you. And straight, too." He emphasized the last with a finger pointed at David.

"Thanks," David said. "I appreciate it. So, I'll see you later, then." He had a reason, a valid reason, to return to see Angelina now. Angelina. A great name. So . . . ethnic.

"What's it all about?" Guido asked. "What for with the questions?"

David was backing out. "Didn't I say?"

"I wasn't interested. Now I am."

He stopped to explain again. "My doctoral thesis. On the Declaration of Independence. It's a comparison on the framers' original intent to establish a government offering liberty and freedom to all, with the reality existing today."

With a tone reserved for the infirm, Guido said, "That's a very nice idea."

David smiled. "Hey! Come on . . . you said you'd be straight."

"It's a very stupid thing for a young man of your age to do. Okay? That straight enough?"

"It'll do," David conceded. "And agreed. On the surface maybe it's a little lame. But it was on the menu for me. My family made out this master game plan two years before I was even born. It had a Ph.D as one of the courses."

"Then I hope this isn't dessert for you."

"No," David said, almost with a sigh. "But I tell you, sometimes I think it's going to be one hell of a long meal."

"It's stupid. A waste of time. All this wondering into what already happened. For what? Over and done with. Things are the way they are. The past is a graveyard of thoughts."

"People learn from the past," David defended.

"Never. People are people. They never change. Dig up any graveyard. You'll never find a new thought, or a person who had not lived his life like the man before him," Guido said, gesturing elaborately with a final sweep of his arm.

The phone rang. Guido mumbled into the receiver, put down the phone, and excused himself to spear a few pickles from a large glass jar. "This is not a waste of time," Guido challenged, slapping a pickle onto some wax paper. "This has to do with life. This pickle is here and now."

"Sold," David proclaimed, and plunked down a dollar. "One piece of the present."

Guido slapped a wrapped pickle into David's hand. "Mugger insurance. The garlic in this is murder. For a month you're protected. A month, at least."

"What about my love life?" David asked, laughing.

"You'll know for sure if it's true love or not."

Chapter Two

On the way home, David found it to be a great pickle, definitely a wise purchase. Guido was probably right about history being a waste of time, as well.

While pickle juice slid down his wrist, he realized how a mediocre day had suddenly, unexpectedly, become a great day. Even his step was lighter as he walked the several blocks through the Village back to his newly leased apartment.

His place was on a tree-lined street with rows of brick and stone buildings. All had more or less identical stoops, whose black iron railings led to single doors. Past the front door of David's building there was a hallway and stairs winding up to the other floors. David's own apartment was on the second floor, which was also home to three other tenants, all of whom he had heard coming and going, and none of whom he had yet seen.

Only after some difficulty with the several locks was he able to gain entrance. The necessity for carrying four keys just to get into his own home seemed, on the surface, excessive. But he had promised his family he would take the necessary precautions to ensure his safety.

It was not, being twenty-eight years old, that he was being treated as a child; but rather that he was being handled as a Winthrop.

Being a Winthrop was a condition, much like a congenital handicap, that he had long since stopped fighting. In some cases, it was best to accede to reality. The familial forces opposing his more flagrant attempts at individuality were far greater than his resources to defend his renegade position.

He was David Jordan Winthrop V, fourth and youngest son of Lydia and David Winston Winthrop of Westport, Connecticut and the international banking community. As he had mentioned to Guido, his destiny had been determined even before he had been born, along with those of his three brothers. Each had been assigned an integral slot to fill in the Winthrop enterprises. David's life blueprint held a liberal arts education at Harvard, to be followed with a Master's in business administration, to be capped off with a Ph.D. in political science.

He had only to complete his dissertation and he would embark on the next stage of the Winthrop Master Plan for Siblings. He was next expected—commanded? sentenced?—to teach at an Ivy League institution of higher learning where he would be expected to distinguish himself as a man of letters; after which post, he would go on to hold a diplomatic position overseas, and eventually he would embark upon a high-level career in American politics.

It was David's own wish that he move into the Village. There he could live like a normal human being, mixing and blending with the general population to gather information on his dissertation. Oddly enough, his parents had been immensely pleased with the idea, seeing as how the Kennedy boys had also seen fit to direct personal attention to domestic poverty projects and investigations into third world tragedies. It was, David's mother claimed, chic to be concerned about the plight of one's fellow human beings.

There was the concern over David's safety, however. But, as David was the least publicized of any of the Winthrop sons, the chances were that dressed in the uniform of the local plebians, very few would separate him from other struggling young doctoral candidates.

Thus the many locks were just one of the precautionary measures to ensure the safety of an heir to one of the world's great banking fortunes.

Inside, the apartment was tastefully decorated in expensive and conservative furnishings: leathers, fine woods, a few good paintings, and built-in shelves to house David's personal library and state-of-the-art stereo components.

He spent the rest of the afternoon assembling a good card file system for his research data. Periodically his thoughts would turn to the mysterious Angelina and his pulse would gallop a bit, his thoughts winding through various libidinous corridors to stir his body until he would be forced to rise from the desk to accomplish some unnecessary physical chore. At seven, he made himself a light dinner, after which he took a brief walk. On the walk, he passed by the Deli Italia.

Standing across the street, hands in his pockets, he remembered a song. It was from *My Fair Lady*. Something about the pavement not staying beneath his feet anymore. Something like that, and that there were lilac trees in the heart of town. But here, there were no blossoms. There were only some dried leaves. But it didn't matter. He had the feel, the sense of there being flowers in the general vicinity of the Deli Italia.

There is a bloody romantic fool in the vicinity of the Deli Italia, that's what, David thought as he moved on. He had gone mad. Maybe it was the moon. He looked up. There was no moon.

By the time he returned home he had talked to himself. It had been a severe man-to-man conversation, in which the bottom line had turned out to be: shape up, cool out, collect yourself. Forget *her*.

At home, chastened, exorcized of his temporary obsession over a strange and cantankerous—although beautiful—young woman, he intended to spend the evening delving into a rare historical document his father had arranged for him to borrow from the Library of Congress.

And he did. For a while.

It was during his deepest point of concentration, while listening to the refrains of Debussy's *La Mer*, that the racket began in the apartment next door.

At first he thought it might end, but the commotion continued for half an hour in fits and starts, which was almost more annoying than the steady banging as it brought up his hopes, only to have them repeatedly dashed.

David sat back and thought about the situation. He had envisioned meeting his neighbors in the hallway. Introductions would be gradual, always warm, tinged with charm. A few agreeable nods might turn into more lengthy encounters, and if there was a basis, perhaps a friendship might ensue.

Instead, a moment later, he stood outside his neighbor's apartment and pounded on the door to be heard above the racket within. He knew now why the papers reported strange murders committed against veritable strangers. *I don't know, Officer. He seemed like such a nice, quiet young man. And then one night...* He would be cool. His parents hated adverse publicity, especially headlines attributing acts of mayhem to their youngest son. He pounded again. This was something, at least— a token act of violence.

A silence followed, then the door swung open with rapid force.

"I'm afraid the noise is—" David stopped. It was Angelina—Angelina of the delicatessen.

For a moment, she, too, seemed surprised. Almost immediately thoughts assembled behind her eyes. Then the thoughts took on a voice. "Look, I have had my share of creeps in this city. So don't ask for trouble, cause you'll find it." She slammed the door in his face.

David listened to a series of locks being secured.

"Wait...uh...look," he called, speaking into the wood. He tried to imagine what she was doing on the other side of the barrier. Listening? Fuming? Calling the police, God forbid. What was she thinking? He had an idea; it wasn't good. "This isn't what you think, Angelina. Angelina? That's your name, isn't it? I know what you're thinking."

"If you did, you'd be a mile away by now," came the muffled voice; the *angry* muffled voice.

David was encouraged. They had set up a dialogue. Now reason would prevail. Five minutes from now, he would be back at his desk with the recent past behind him, and the distant past of American political history spread out neatly before him. There would be peace. "You're thinking I followed you back here..." David laughed, relaxing as the full absurdity of the situation hit him. "Which isn't the case. Actually I'm your—"

"Buzz off!" came the voice from within the apartment. The hammering took up again; this time with a marked vengeance behind each swing.

"Will you listen? Angelina! I live next door! I'm a neighbor. Your neighbor. In Apartment E. David Winthrop's my name. Check it out, ask the landlady! Our landlady!"

There was a break in the hammering. "Anyone can read a name on a mailbox! Get away!"

"This is stupid. I've got identification." Now he was getting angry.

Across the hallway, a man in a plaid bathrobe stepped out and scowled. "I'm calling the cops, buddy!" He, too, slammed the door.

"Oh, no..." David moved rapidly to the man's door and knocked. "I'm afraid there's been a mistake, here. You—and Angelina, across the hall—don't seem to understand that I—"

"They're on their way!" came the response from the other side of the door. "They're gonna nail you good, buddy!"

"Oh, nice... great, fine," David said, standing between the two apartments and speaking to no one but himself. "This is crazy. I live here," he explained to the air.

He took his frustration back to his apartment and downed a couple of aspirin. The pounding next door continued, although it slackened off just about the time he heard the police in the hallway. For a moment, David cringed, a sense of panic arising. It was ridiculous; he was being treated like a criminal. Furious, himself, he stepped into the hall and faced the two uniformed officers who were speaking to the man in the plaid bathrobe.

"That's him!" the man said, pointing a beefy finger in David's direction.

"Officer, my name is David Winthrop," he began evenly. "And I live here. I've been trying to tell them, but some sort of hysteria seems to have set in. I just recently moved, you see. So it's natural and understandable that no one knows me yet. I believe in exercising caution as much as the next guy, but in all due respect, I think we're . . . they're . . . being a little overreactive." The cops and his neighbor were staring at him without expression. Gamely, he went on. "This all began because there was a lot of racket next door and I went to ask if she—" David hitched his head in the direction of Angelina's door "—could maybe hold it down a little. Only she . . . well, she got the wrong idea."

The police went to Angelina's door. She opened it a moment later. She was wearing black tights and a long red sweater. A bandanna was wrapped around her head, giving her an exotic look, both gamine and sensual.

"Do you know this man?" the police asked her.

Angelina frowned, casting a disgusted, sloe-eyed look David's way.

David nodded amiably. "Hello again."

Angelina ignored him. "Know him? No. I don't know him. I saw him today, that's all. In a store where I work. We talked briefly. Briefly." She looked at David, then back to the police. "He must have followed me home. It's not the first time it's happened with guys. And I could have handled it," she finished indignantly.

"For crissakes, I live here!" David shouted.

The police tensed, ready to apprehend the maniac in their midst. David calmed himself. In a quieter tone, he went on. "Okay, okay. I can prove it. Identification. Lease—in my desk drawer. Look, this is ridiculous," he exploded again. "It's just a crazy coincidence us living here. But that's true, what she said. I *did* meet her today. In an Italian deli. She was beating up on some guy. And she's damn right, she could have handled this. One hand tied behind her back." Looking to Angelina, he said, "And that's not necessarily a point in your favor, dear."

But of course it really was. A picture of that meeting flashed through his mind. Like distinct echoes, the feelings associated with the vision filled him once again with that initial sense of excitement to have met a creature of such mercurial temperament. He cast a quick glance to Angelina.

Her face was darkly placid—the way a hurricane sky appears just before the fury is unleashed. He could scarcely claim a past with her to look back on, but already history had taken on rosier hues than that of the present. He returned his attention to the officers. "I swear to you, I had no idea she was living next door to me."

Their expressions showed a disinclination to trust in his oath-taking.

It took a few more minutes, a few more crazy minutes, and the police were finally convinced of his story.

Disappointment filled the air. He was not some sort of ripper or slasher or masher, after all.

"Sorry," he said, with the mock, sweeping bow of a flamboyant stage actor taking his curtain call. "Hate to let you all down. I'm just your basic ordinary decent American citizen. Name's David. It's been real swell meeting all you nice folk. Let's do it again real soon. Maybe have a potluck on the stairs—relive good times, that sort of thing? What are neighbors for, anyway?"

The small gathering of other tenants living in the building gaped from the hall and stairs and down the stairwell as David closed his door and retreated, at last, from chaos to sanity. His last image of the outer world before shutting himself away was of the beautiful, mysterious, aggravating Angelina. Scowling.

The following afternoon, he returned from the library to find a small package wrapped in gift paper outside his door. Taking it inside, he found the present to be a can of mixed nuts. A small piece of white paper affixed to the can's top, read, "Welcome to the second floor. Angelina."

At first he was pleased. It was nice, cute—the idea of the nuts. He figured the nuts were a kind of symbolic gesture, a witty summing up of the whole incident.

Maybe, that is.

On the other hand, he might very well be giving his illusive neighbor too much credit. Perhaps the nuts meant nothing more to her than that they were just a bunch of nuts in a can.

After considering the matter, he decided to remain distant. After the social debacle in the hall, it wouldn't hurt his sense of dignity any to remain a bit aloof for a while. Otherwise he might have gone over and suggested she stop by for a glass of wine. The image in his mind was clear: two warring tribesmen laying down their spears. Ha! And Guido thought people could never learn, never progress!

Guido, David thought darkly, is a wise man.

A part of him—make that a big part of him—would have liked to have seen Angelina again. Even after the hall incident, he had remained intrigued. To talk to her, to find out about her, still loomed as an attractive, if unlikely, prospect.

Of course, God only knows he would also have had to invite the squealer in the bathrobe. Otherwise there would be the risk of arousing suspicion. Speculation would abound that he had other than the highest gentlemanly motives.

Not, mind you, that he didn't harbor a thought or two in the general direction of the bedroom; but thoughts were not deeds. His only crime was male fantasy.

If she *did* come over and they imbibed in a drink or two or three, perhaps she would loosen up. David's mind pursued the scenario. In fifteen minutes he could learn everything there was to know about her; and there the whole matter of Angelina would neatly end.

He would discover that she was just a woman like any other; one attractive female like a hundred others who had passed through his life. The obsession would dissolve and he could go about his life in peace—and on schedule.

Now, wait: did he hear the word "obsession"?

Yes. He did. *Obsession.* And it was true; marginally, anyway. He had been thinking of her off and on ever since he had seen her in the Deli Italia.

And, of course, it was ridiculous. He was a grown man, a man with important things to accomplish. Some people, many people, even considered him to be important. He was a man, as the song said, with the world on a string. Ask him and he'd hum the entire tune. Only somehow he had inadvertently become entangled in another string attached to this Angelina person. Well, that was simple enough to remedy: he would sever the connection.

With feelings of raw vindication, he threw the can of nuts into the kitchen garbage can. There, the deed was done. The matter over. *Fini.*

A half hour later he made another pass through the kitchen, retrieved the nuts, and placed them in his cupboard. There was no sense in being wasteful. They were perfectly decent nuts.

Chapter Three

Angelina had not given the can of nuts another thought, once having deposited it at the door of her new neighbor. The nuts had been on sale. They were meant simply as a civilized gesture of goodwill; nothing more.

Her mind, on that late afternoon after she had returned from her dancing class, was firmly rooted upon the pressing matter of her ballet career.

Only two hours ago, the great, the noble, the incomparable Sasha Petrovsky, had visited her class unannounced. He had come to visit his old friend, a man who had been his own teacher years ago in Russia and who now instructed Angelina's class. Both men had defected from their native country. It was an exciting and touching moment for Angelina and the other students to watch the two legends embrace. Sasha, himself, led a portion of their class.

And afterward...afterward! Angelina closed her eyes, feeling once again the exhilaration of that moment pulse through her body.

Sasha Petrovsky had complimented her. He had even asked if she were not Russian, perhaps. "Perhaps," she had replied, flushing as pink as her silk toe shoes. God only knew she was a bit of everything else; why not Russian, as well?

In truth, her family's roots were spread like a thin film over the entire globe. Gypsies for countless generations, they had migrated over every inch of Europe, and a faction had even, more recently, established themselves tentatively in America. Her own mother—deceased—had been born in France; her father was Spanish, thus the last name, Zarsuela. But there was a Hungarian grandmother, and her brothers were Italian and Spanish.

It was, Angelina suspected, this confusing stew of bloodlines that had created the hodgepodge of passionate personalities. Although she loved her family, she wanted no more familial entanglements. Her family was incorrigible. She wished only to extricate herself from their web of perpetual intrigues and petty criminal activities.

It was also her father's wish that she rise above her background. Ah, she loved him. Adored him! Zoltan.

He had always believed in her, had always wanted the very best for her. In her desk were three boxes of cherished letters from him written over the years. In these letters he had penned encouraging words for her to continue her formal studies and to practice her ballet. He had also told her of his own dreams for a beautiful life. He was a Gypsy king, yet he wanted more for his people than to wander the globe like ragtag bandits.

In the old days the life of their band had had its good points, so her father claimed. So romantic and colorful it was then! The freedom, the excitement of surviving from day to day by one's wits. But with the advent of police computers, and due to the very lack of space in which his people might roam unmolested by the more civilized factions of society, the life of the Gypsy had lost its glamour.

Over the years her father had embarked on various endeavors to secure a more legitimate place for himself and his people in the mainstream of life. But, for one reason or the other, all his enterprises had soured. But five years ago, fortune had smiled upon her father. At last a successful venture had taken root in the soil of Spain. Zoltan had secured a vineyard. A case of the wine had been sent to her every year. Angelina kept the latest gray wooden crate with Zarsuela Vineyards stamped on its exterior—looking to her like a magestic coat of arms belonging to a great and noble family—in her apartment. On it was a picture of her father. A glance at it was always reassuring; *things could get better.* Here was proof that it was possible to pull one's self out of muck and mire and scale the mountain.

Angelina wanted to dance. This had been her dream for her entire life, or at least from the time she was ten years old and had been sent back to Europe at her father's request to perform in a new traveling circus he had put together. The circus was comprised entirely of Gypsies, different bands coming together to lend their talents to Zoltan's latest vision. There were jugglers and horsemen, acrobats and trapeze artists, acts working with wild animals, fortune-tellers and sideshows and games of chance outside of the main tent.

Up until the Spanish vineyard, the circus was perhaps the longest lasting of any of the Zarsuela family's attempts at legitimate business. But, alas, after two years the circus was disbanded by the authorities of several different countries. There had been too many complaints of robberies and various other petty misdemeanors occurring in towns during the stay of the circus. Incensed, Zoltan had objected strenuously—too strenuously, perhaps—and a full-scale war had developed between the Gypsies and the local citizens. The citizens had won.

Angelina had been returned to America to live with a semirespectable aunt and uncle in Boston. Fortunately, or unfortunately, depending on point of view, the deportation came after she had already tasted the thrill of dancing before an admiring circus audience. She had worn a beautiful dress, appearing like a princess before the crowds of hundreds, and had danced to the live refrains of a Gypsy band playing Hungarian music. In the true tradition of the Zarsuelas she, too, was a fraud, no better than an artistic con artist. Her steps were cleverly improvised. Like any Gypsy worth her heritage, she was a born mimic, and with little trouble she produced a credible performance as a fledgling ballerina.

To be a dancer was, in Angelina's mind, The Exit from the questionable existence of her ancestors and The Entrance into a lofty world of beauty and innocence, where life would take on the gracious form of moving poetry.

Now, sitting on the floor of her apartment, Angelina lost herself in the memory of the words spoken to her that afternoon.

Before leaving their class, Sasha had said, "You have the makings of a prima ballerina. I do not say this often. But I say it now. To *you*." And then, in the stone silence of the room, with all eyes upon her, Sasha Petrovsky had said, "You will to come and to dance with my new company."

Like a genie, like some magical wizard of wondrous good fortune, he had swept from the room, evaporating, but leaving her wish intact.

Her teacher stopped her as she was preparing to float home. He told her, "Of course Sasha is correct. You have great gifts. You can one day be famous. You *will*."

Angelina's heart had soared, looped, spiraled.

Now, still dizzy with joy, she sat on her bare wooden floor, which was polished to a high luster, and counted out the money she had saved. It wasn't much, but if she were frugal it would cover her living expenses while she was to rehearse with Sasha's new group. Ballet might be beautiful and classy, but dancing in a disco would undoubtedly pay more until she did, indeed, become the Pavlova of her generation.

A shadow of sadness dimmed her mood. This was a new beginning, but also an ending. And the finish of anything was always disconcerting to Angelina. She had been forced to leave too many things behind, too many lovely places and good people and good times. And tomorrow? Angelina sighed. Tomorrow she would have to tell Guido that she was leaving the deli. Her time with the pickles had ended.

The money was kept in a thin leather pouch, handed down to her from her mother's mother's mother's mother. It had housed the secret funds of all these previous generations, and now it contained the sum of twenty-five hundred dollars belonging to her. To keep money in the bank was simply not in her nature. She was, in spite of herself, still a product of her environment, and a Gypsy's philosophy of commerce did not include trust of legalized institutions, such as federally insured banks. One kept money where it could be instantly tapped. There was always the possibility that a midnight flight could materialize, whether or not one was responsible or innocent of a crime committed. To be a Gypsy was to be suspect; the two conditions were synonymous.

But soon, soon, Angelina sighed, holding the money tight against her heart, she would be a dancer. And *that* was synonymous with all that was fine and beautiful in the world.

She looked around the room, trying to rectify her fantastic vision of the future with present reality. There was little enough to see. One wall was partially covered in mirrored squares, bought square by square, and affixed to the wall with a backing of sticky tape. A ballet barre ran the length of the mirrored section. The installation of the barre had necessitated the previous night's pounding. There was a small kitchen, with very little cupboard space, a single chest of drawers, a rickety table with three mismatched chairs, a low Oriental platform, functioning both as bed and couch, with throw pillows for the backrest, and an open door leading to a small bathroom.

There was also, like a shrine, her father's wine crate. Zoltan Zarsuela's proud and somewhat mischievous countenance faced her from across the room. He had done something wonderful. And so would she.

Rehearsals began. Each new day was exhilarating and exhausting. It was not only that she was testing her physical and artistic prowess, she was also expanding her sense of what she could expect from the world.

Previously, anything good had only lasted so long. Invariably the joy and satisfaction had been snatched out from under her by what Angelina had come to think of as cosmic manipulation by unseen forces. She had almost begun to relax into the harmony of her present existence when a mysterious and terrible event shattered her tenuous new sense of reality.

It happened five weeks into rehearsals.

She had come home to her apartment, tendons aching, a slight stitch in her side, but otherwise feeling pleased with her performance that day. Sasha had not exactly said it, not in words anyway, but a person would have had to have been deaf and dumb not to see that he found her as good as the company's leading female dancer.

After she showered, she took out some frozen fish sticks, and was replacing the remainder back in the small freezer compartment when she noted the crinkle in the small foil-wrapped packet positioned next to the pint of chocolate ice cream.

For a moment she did nothing. Awareness flushed through her system, all nerve endings seeming to speak in one unanimous voice at once. The message was the same. But the packet she had left so smooth-surfaced and shiny was not the same anymore.

She pulled it out and took it to the counter to unwrap the contents. But even before she did, she knew the truth. The money was gone.

When the foil was pulled away, not money, but strips of torn newspaper were emptied from the antique pouch.

A sick feeling washed over her. Light-headed, she stood where she was. She had never fainted before, but she felt that she actually might now. Tears came to her eyes and she began to sob uncontrollably.

Her money! Her money that she had worked so hard to save. The small amount of cash was all she had to support her enormous dream of freedom from the past...freedom to be herself...freedom to create a beautiful destiny. The ragged scraps of paper mocked her dream.

The rest of the evening she sat on her bed, not sleeping but merely staring around her room, wondering what she was going to do now besides starve to death. She had no money and she had to use all her time to rehearse, so she couldn't work.

How could the theft have happened? As distracted and tired as she had been lately from the grueling rehearsal schedule, she had nevertheless always kept the money hidden, and had always made sure to lock her door. Having been raised among thieves, there were certain precautions one took as a matter of course. Angelina systematically surveyed the situation. There was no sign of forced entry. There was no sign of anything having been touched in her entire place.

When morning came she dragged herself out of bed with the knowledge that she could pick one of three alternatives: she could starve, or steal—which she would have died before doing!—or beg.

She begged.

With an expression reflecting white-hot fury, Guido Rufio listened to Angelina's story of the missing money. When she was finished, he said nothing. He disappeared into the back storeroom and returned with two enormous empty boxes. Then, as Angelina watched, he flung canned goods and cheeses and pastas and jars of pickles and frozen products into the boxes.

When Angelina protested his generosity, Guido said, "So am I supposed to bring my family to see a ballerina, or a skeleton dance?"

For the rest of her rehearsal schedule, Angelina had enough salamis to feed the entire troupe, pasta to feed all of Little Italy for half a year, and the smell of Guido's famous garlic-soaked pickles developed into a living presence in her apartment.

For David Winthrop, the two months since he had moved into the Greenwich Village apartment had come and gone with the briskness of the fall weather. With concentrated effort he had all but completed his doctoral thesis, and was beginning to have intimations of becoming a real person again. His days of molehood were almost at their end. That Friday night he was even going to hang out with his buddies. They were going to take in a basketball game and who knew what else later? A leisurely pizza and beer maybe, the stuff of real life!

With pizza and basketball happily on his horizon, he was zipping around his apartment, enjoying the third movement of Beethoven's Symphony Number Seven, when the sound of the phone joined the orchestration.

He could tell by the ring that it was his mother. It had her vibration, if such a thing were possible. He also knew what she would want. Determined and energetic, his mother was Queen of the Appointment Book. David had often thought her sole reason to live was to schedule people's lives into the squares of her master calendar.

"David, so glad to catch you home," she said upon hearing his voice.

"I was just going out."

"Going out is precisely why I called."

"Why did I suspect that?"

"Because you're clever and intuitive. Like your mother, darling."

"Then your extraordinary powers of perception may have already told you that I am not going to—"

"The ballet tonight."

"To the ballet tonight."

"You must, David. Something's come up and no one else from the family can attend."

"Need I remind you . . . this week—at your behest, Mother—I have already gone to two of the most deadly cultural affairs ever known to mankind."

"David, we have gone over this a thousand times."

"And you still don't get it, Mother. I am not a piece of furniture to be shipped here and there to make your life or anyone else's life, more comfortable. I'm going to a basketball game."

"David—"

"I know. It's my fate and duty as a Winthrop to wither and die in a museum, or drown when I fall asleep face-down in a glass of Dom Perignon at one of your infernal cocktail parties for little-known causes. If I were Catholic, I'd have been canonized six months ago."

"David! I'm hurt."

"No, you aren't, Mother. It would take a neutron explosion to put a dent in your spirits."

"I need you to help me. And you will. You must."

"I must." He sighed resignedly. At least he had spoken his piece. It wasn't like he went down without a fight. The problem was, he understood his mother's point of view. How could he not? The social conditioning had begun at his first burp. In banking circles, it was thought to be prudent to dole out bits and pieces of time and money and seeming enthusiasm to struggling proletariate enterprises. So spake his mother. When a family was richer than Croesus, it was never wise to appear unfeeling and greedy before the eyes of the public. As a reminder, David's mother kept a picture of the ill-fated Marie Antoinette in her dressing room.

"So. What smile-and-simper affair is it to be this time?" he asked as he sank, defeated once again, into his desk chair. "An extravaganza for a group who's donated time to the spiritual upliftment of people with fallen arches?"

"Don't be cute, David. But you're close. About the feet part, anyway. As I said, it's the ballet."

David moaned. "I was hoping you weren't serious."

"And you'll adore Melissa."

"Melissa?"

"Darling, this is crucial to your father. Melissa Segers is the daughter of Charles Segers. She was utterly thrilled when she heard you'd be taking her."

"*Chicky* Segers? Old light fingers?" David thought back to the not too distant past and smiled. Chicky Segers was a former ambassador to a South American banana republic now owing a lot of money to the Winthrop bank. It was more or less common knowledge that Chicky Segers had, with the help of certain unscrupulous native government officials, made off with more than his share of the proceeds of the money meant to be used in development projects for the country. Although living in Bermuda, Chicky still maintained a certain amount of leverage in the nation, and it didn't take a genius IQ to figure out that the Winthrops hoped

Chicky might apply his favored position to the bank's benefit.

"It would be nice if you could be attentive."

"The most I can promise is that I'll do my best to stay awake during the performance."

"There's to be a thing afterward," Lydia Winthrop said, her voice now dripping with honey as she knew very well that she was pushing her prerogative of motherhood to the far limits.

"A thing."

"Something nice for the cast. The right people will be there. And, of course, the press, David. Your father donated quite a lovely chunk of money to this troupe, so it's important that you get your face in as many shots as possible. Just to remind people."

So the basketball tickets were parted with.

The two guys he was to have gone with invited a third in David's place. They came by just as David was about to leave. He was dressed in a black tuxedo and they were dressed in sweatshirts.

"This a funeral tonight or a date?" one of them asked, backing out of the apartment while doing a pretend dribble with an imaginary basketball.

"I should think that would be perfectly obvious," David said. "A funeral. My own. Third one this week."

As he stood in the doorway he heard a rattling sound to his right and his heart momentarily and unaccountably took flight. The noise was emanating from the apartment of Angelina Zarsuela.

Whatever his friend was saying was totally lost to David. His undivided attention was directed to the vision who appeared in the hall, and who was presently drifting past him in a cloud of pale pink glitter.

Angelina's hair was worn up in a tightly wrapped coil; she looked delicate as a doe, sophisticated as a Parisian model, and desirable as any woman David could imagine. He hadn't seen her, really seen her, this close in a couple of months. And on those occasions when he had caught the barest glimpse of her, she was always hurrying along, wearing jeans and bundled up to the neck in scarves and down to the nose with stocking caps.

Now she wore this dress, this long, clinging piece of pink cloth that shimmered with billions of tiny beads as she moved past him. On her arm she carried a wool shawl, inappropriate to the outfit and undoubtedly unsuitable for the time of year.

His lust changed immediately to concern as he understood that the dress must have been borrowed for some splendid occasion in her life, and that having nothing appropriate to wear over the dress, she had chosen the flimsy covering, rather than appear a spectacle in her everyday coat. David thought of his mother and her friends with their many furs.

Angelina's progress past him was slowed by the presence of his friends in her way.

"Hello," David said softly, with uncustomary shyness, as she was just in front of him.

She looked at him, or maybe just through him. "Hi."

And then just as suddenly as she had appeared, she was gone.

"Who the hell was that?" asked David's friend, who had stopped bouncing the imaginary ball to follow Angelina with his eyes.

"The Princess of the Second Floor," David said.

"I'm in love." His friend swooned, falling against the wall and sliding down to his haunches.

"Yeah," David said. "That happens sometimes."

* * *

Melissa Segers, Chicky Segers's daughter, was a bland drink of water who had come down from graduate school in Boston for the occasion, the occasion being the Carnegie Hall opening of Sasha Petrovsky's new troupe.

As it happened, David had no trouble remaining alert throughout the entire performance of Sasha's gala presentation of leaping and strutting soldiers and spinning, flying, and, eventually, dying maidens.

Upon opening the program, his eyes skimmed the list of cast members and although, he supposed later, the name might have made an impression on some subliminal level, it was not until he saw her on the stage that he recognized Angelina Zarsuela as being The Angelina Zarsuela of the Second Floor.

For more than two and half hours, plus intermission, David sat mesmerized, either watching the most beautiful woman in the world leap and twirl and glide across the stage, or waiting for the most beautiful woman in the world to leap and twirl and glide across the stage. The truth was, it would not have mattered if she had just sat there; he was that impressed, that taken with the woman. Apparently everyone else in the audience felt similarly.

After the last curtain call, David fought his way, with Melissa Segers in breathless tow, to the stage door. Here he was apprehended by two security guards. No one was to enter the backstage. Sasha Petrovsky was a defector, after all, and defectors could not be too careful.

In the rented limousine, on the way to the opening-night bash, Melissa Segers whined that she was tired of crowds. She was tired of going to boring, pointless things just because her father said it was the right thing to do. What she really wanted, she said, breathing against David's neck, was to go somewhere quiet with him and spend a few meaningful hours together.

"Melissa," David said, furrowing his brow, "I'm terribly surprised at this attitude of yours. I not only look forward to doing my part for my family's honor, but I consider it my privilege. I wouldn't dream of missing out on tonight's party. It's simply," he said, "unthinkable that I wouldn't be there. You aren't really very culturally minded, are you, Melissa?"

Melissa Seger looked at him, baffled. David smiled and kissed her fingertips lightly. "Don't fight destiny, Melissa. That's what I always say."

Chapter Four

Angelina was not the official female star of the troupe, yet that was how she felt as she wafted along on a stream of ecstasy. If only her father could be with her! If only Zoltan could have seen her tonight!

Instead, Guido Rufio and Lila, his daughter, hugged her and cried with her and told her that she had been the most beautiful, the most talented, the most phenomenal of all on stage that night. And, somehow, Angelina herself knew that it was not just the idle praise of the near and dear. It was a fact. She had It; she, Angelina Zarsuela, had the indefinable but recognizable *It*.

The party for the cast and those well-heeled patrons of the arts who had contributed money and social influence to making Sasha's vision into a reality, was held in the Park Avenue penthouse of a magazine mogul. There were almost as many waiters in attendance as guests. Food on silver platters was exhibited like splendid art arrangements in the huge dining room. No one's glass was empty of champagne for more than thirty seconds. Angelina felt as if she had stepped into a fairyland.

Whatever she touched, whatever she tasted, whatever sight her eyes fell upon, she shared it in her heart with Zoltan. She was standing by a window, looking down upon the lights of the city displayed before her like a carpet strewn with jewels—and feeling secretly that each gem was there for her to take—when a voice said, "You were right. You *will* be a legend."

Angelina turned and found herself staring blankly at someone she knew but couldn't remember. And then she did. "You..." she said with a start, at a loss for his name.

"David. David Winthrop."

"Sorry," Angelina said hastily, and skittered her eyes away from his to search for an escape route into the crowd. There was something about him. She was already uncomfortable beneath the green scrutiny of his eyes.

"Don't be," David said easily. "It's happened to me before, too. Even with a good friend. Now that's bad. You don't expect to see them somewhere. And there they are, out of context. So they don't register."

"Excuse me," she said, and started to go.

"No," David said, and gently took hold of her elbow. Her skin was warm. He did not want to let go of her; he was enjoying the momentary contact, smelling the scent of her perfume. For a second his good judgment seemed in jeopardy of being totally obliterated by a sudden rush of desire. He felt like crushing her against him, felt like entering her, filling her with himself. He loosened his hold on her, alarmed when he suddenly realized his grip had turned tight enough to leave prints. Noises from the party surrounded them, but seemed not to enter the space they shared together. "I won't excuse you," he said in a voice dry and forced from his state of arousal. "I'm curious. I want to know why you dislike me so much."

She seemed surprised, either by his bluntness or by the statement itself.

"I wasn't aware that I do." Angelina rubbed her arm distractedly.

David was relieved she said nothing about it and he went on, glad to avoid another complication in their relationship. "Well, then, maybe dislike's the wrong word. Maybe it's that you feel uncomfortable around me."

"I don't even think of you," Angelina returned.

She was beginning to feel jittery, as if she had to bolt right then and there or something terrible was going to happen. Each second that she remained in his presence she felt as if she were being bound tighter by invisible silken threads. She felt as if she were being captured slowly and methodically. Her heart was beating too fast. Her head felt light. Still, she couldn't withdraw. The party itself seemed a distant event made insignificant by the green eyes looking down at her. From the very first time, they had filled her with a kind of fear. But the danger was at the same time tantalizing in the pleasure it brought.

A shadowy exhilaration passed through her. When she was very young, too young to know exactly why they were running, she had felt this same joyous abandon of living on the edge of life when Zoltan and her brothers would make a dash through city and countryside. It was a wonderful game to them, life was! Or *their* sense of life, anyway. She had finally come to see their view of the world as childish and decidedly slanted. Her attention drew back to her neighbor standing before her as his voice interrupted her memories.

"Well, at least you thought of me once. At least long enough to give me a gift. I never thanked you for the nuts. So thank you—officially."

"What?"

"The nuts?"

"What nuts?"

"You don't remember."

"No. I don't."

"You look very beautiful," David said.

She was thinking that he was probably the most attractive man at the party. He wore his formal attire as if born in it. The sandy hair, the subtle cleft in his chin, the extraordinary green of his eyes, and the smile...the physical trappings of the blessed. He was an animal on his own turf. Another smile like that, another once-over from the green eyes, and she would be easy prey.

"I really must go. I see Sasha..." Angelina looked past David to her ballet director. Sasha Petrovsky was circulating the party, dressed in a splendid dark blue crushed-velvet jacket.

"It was October, when you gave me the nuts," David said, continuing on as if they were involved in a gripping conversation of tremendous import to the both of them.

"October, you say? That's...that's...really not important to me, you know?"

"Well, we always have such splendid talks."

"I'm going," Angelina announced again, but made no move to leave. He just kept on as if everything was perfectly normal between them.

"So in October, I was surprised, you see, to return home and find this can of nuts outside my door. With a note. From you—as you already know. It was, I suppose, meant to be a peace offering of sorts, after the war in the hall."

A clear picture of that night flashed before Angelina. Along with that picture came other scenes from her past, flickering through her mind with the speed of cards being shuffled. David Winthrop was a reminder of the old world, which held countless disappointments and humiliations and uncertainties. She had this one night to live in the brightness of her own personal triumph. And here he was, like a stain on a white carpet. She had not wanted to recognize him. If she could erase him, she would. But, instead, there he stood with that half smile and those green eyes that seemed to be peering around the corners of her mind.

"Excuse me, David, but what is it, exactly, that you want from me? Because I definitely get the feeling that you aren't going to leave me alone until you get it."

"What I want?" David rocked back on his heels and looked through the window where the lights of New York City twinkled like fallen stars. The question seemed to catch him off guard, and also to intrigue him. "What I want?" he said again, clearing his voice afterward, like a boy in class about to recite a poem. Then he looked back to her. "It's about the nuts. The nuts are the whole issue here. And I think the best thing to do is for us just to face the situation head on and be done with it." He paused. "They've never been sampled, the nuts haven't."

"Yes?" Angelina said. In her hand she held a small pink beaded purse that matched her gown. She tapped it against her side. "You must have a plan, of course."

"True. I do. They've been aging, the nuts have. Like wine. And I thought..."

At the mention of wine a wave of sweet melancholy filled Angelina. *Wine.* Her father... her father! How terribly proud he would have been of her this night. And how much he would have loved the party with all the wonderful flowers and food and people in their splendid gowns and tuxedos. Oh, yes! She and Zoltan would have laughed and cried over their mutual triumphs. He would have played the balalaika and she would have danced. Together they would have drunk his wine. *Viva!* To life! They had escaped their destinies. On the surface, at least, they were Gypsies no more.

"...the neighborly thing would be to have you share them with me, these aged nuts. Maybe you could drop by later on if you're too strung out to sleep. I've never had the opportunity to eat nuts with a legend."

"Then I'm afraid you're going to have to wait a bit longer. Because, unfortunately, I'm not a legend. Yet," she said.

In the form of a silent touch, David gave a single downward nod. Offering an additional half smile, he said, "Then, I'll wait. If I can age nuts, I can wait for legends to be created."

Behind Angelina a voice cried out. "My beauty, there are you! Not to stand on the side, my flower. Come, come! Into the center of the sun! Where you belong!" Sasha spun around in a circle, his crushed-blue-velveteen arms shimmering like rays of sunlight.

"That man seems to be looking our way. It's rare I'm called a flower," David said, "so I suppose he means you."

The bodies of the rich and famous and infamous parted as Angelina moved to where Sasha stood waiting. The master dancer had full control of his renowned penetrating Russian stare as he looked down at Angelina and said in a voice meant to be heard by the one hundred or so guests, "You will someday be the most famous ballerina in this world."

Then he kissed her hand. There were sighs all about.

But when Angelina looked up, it was past Sasha Petrovsky and into the eyes of David Winthrop, who was standing alone by the window with a champagne glass in his hand. When their eyes met, he lifted the glass to her.

She could not be certain, but if she read the amusement behind his eyes correctly, he might have been saying something like, "Destiny calls." Of course, she couldn't be certain. But it did seem like something he would come up with.

The rest of the evening it annoyed her that she had chosen that particular moment to look over at him. She hadn't meant to; she didn't even know why she had. But now he'd suppose that she had deliberately sought him out, and he'd suspect—erroneously—that he was important to her.

To make matters even worse, she saw him leave soon afterward in the company of a slender young woman with pale hair. The departure precluded any further opportunity for her to deliberately ignore him, and thus put matters straight.

Four hours later, Angelina stood in the middle of her apartment. All thoughts of the performance, the party, the adulation, and David Winthrop had fled her mind in the face of her current situation.

There was something wrong. She could sense it in the atmosphere, the ''wrongness.''

Shivering from the sensation, she initially tried to convince herself that it was the cold on her bare arms. But her finely honed instincts told her otherwise. Beneath all thoughts, the single word ''trouble'' repeated.

Oh, please, God . . . don't let anything ruin tonight. Tonight, dear God, tonight was the beginning for me . . . the night I have waited for my entire life. When no lightning flashed, and no voice spoke, she took the hint that she was, at least for the time being, on her own in the current situation. God, like most of the other residents of New York City, must have been sleeping.

As calmly as possible, Angelina mentally retraced her movements since she had returned home.

She had entered the apartment and taken off her wrap. Still wearing the pink beaded gown, she was halfway across the room when she noticed that the crate containing the wine had been slightly moved from its usual position.

But how could that be? The door was locked when she had entered. The window, she saw, was likewise down and—

The window was down, but the lock was no longer in place.

Like lasers, Angelina's eyes surveyed the rest of the room, taking in every detail as she had remembered leaving it, and finding no changes but for the crate and the window. There was one absolute certainty in all of this: someone had come and gone from her apartment. And whoever it was, could come back.

Quickly she ran to her dresser and threw in a change of clothing, plus a nightgown; then ran to the bathroom and collected toiletries she would need. It was late, but she'd find a cab and take it to the Rufios' home. Out of conditioning, she could not bring herself to call the police. The police had never been friends to the Gypsies. No people were friend to Gypsies—an axiom drummed into her since childhood.

Angelina took care to lock the door after her, and she was hurrying past David Winthrop's door when he suddenly appeared coming up the stairs from the first floor.

They both stopped at once; Angelina, because she at first had thought it might be whoever had broken in once that night, returning; David because he was slightly inebriated and thought that he might only be imagining a terrified Angelina holding a suitcase in one hand, standing before his apartment door at three in the morning.

Seeing it was only David, Angelina started forward again. David hadn't yet moved when the crash sounded from Angelina's apartment.

Both turned in the direction of the sound.

"Oh, God..." Angelina breathed out. "Oh, no..."

"What was that?" David asked, sensing, even through the haze of too many cocktails, that something wasn't at all right.

"I don't know," Angelina said, the words coming out in a long slow breath as she tried not to panic. "He...they...whoever...must have been in there when I—"

"Who do you think it could be, Angelina?" David had quickly come up beside her. He held her small shoulders as he looked past her to the closed door of her apartment.

"I don't know," she whispered and looked up into his eyes. David read terror in their dark depths. He almost managed to smile, noting that she was human after all. "I don't know," she repeated.

David would never know what took possession of him at that moment. Perhaps it was the feel of her body, fragile and feminine; perhaps it had only been the liquor in his blood distorting reality; perhaps it was some primal male territorial hormone called up from his genetic past. Whatever it was, David found himself suddenly slamming his shoulder against Angelina's door. Angelina was at his side, unlocking the door even as he battered against it.

He rushed into the apartment first, with Angelina after him, just as the dark silhouette of a man slid beyond the windowsill and dropped out of view.

David flew across the room and, looking out the escape route, saw nothing but black night.

"Gone," he reported, turning to Angelina. "Fast bastard, wasn't he?"

She was standing with her head down, breathing in deeply, trying to calm herself. It had been a long time since she had lived with the constant awareness of her people that at any time there might be a reason to run or to protect oneself from imminent danger. Being ready dulled the fear as the threat arose; but she was no longer in tune with the ways the Gypsy used to survive, and this night she felt the sharp claws of terror rip at her insides.

"Come on," David said, putting his arm around her shoulder. "You're staying with me tonight."

"No."

"Yes," David insisted. "You're meant to be a ballerina, not a street fighter, Angelina."

Her first impulse was to explode that she was a Gypsy! She could take care of any sneaking, thieving rat who came into her private space in the dead of the night! But this old ritualized sense of honor was no match for her desire to discard the taint of her heritage. If anything, at that moment, she felt like sobbing—not out of fear so much as out of confusion. Who was she, what was she, really, after all?

So Angelina said nothing. Her eyes grew misty and, amazingly, a pool of tears formed where defiance had so recently lodged. *She was a ballerina.* She didn't have to fight or run or hide or offer any kind of excuse anymore. *She was a ballerina.* She kept repeating the phrase as a mantra.

No resistance was offered as David guided her into the hall. She picked up her suitcase, and David took it from her. "I'll take the couch tonight," he said.

"No," Angelina refused, but this time without hostility. "Thanks, anyway. But I can't stay with you. I've a friend, I'll go there."

"It's late, Angelina. Besides, I'm a friend, too," he said. "Or I'd like to be."

"It wouldn't be right," Angelina said looking away, "...me staying."

"Yeah, what would the bozo in the bathrobe think? He'd probably get the National Guard out after me." He waited a beat, and with more seriousness said, "Look at it this way. It wouldn't have been exactly right that I end up dead meat in there, either. But sometimes you just have to go with the situation as it presents itself. Believe it or not, life usually works out." He brushed away a line of tears marching slow-motion down Angelina's face. "What's this?" he said, gently drawing her chin around. "Concern over a hero's close call?"

"Just tired," she said with a sniff. Embarrassed, she tried to blink away the tears.

"Nah," David said as he backed away toward his door with her suitcase. "You're scared. Like any other normal human being would be." He unlocked the door and held it open wide for her. She was still standing in the hall, her face wet, her eyes filled with hesitation. "You don't have to be afraid of me, Angelina. I'm a hero, remember? A hero lives by a strict code of honor when it comes to damsels in distress."

He could smell her perfume as she moved past him into his apartment. For a moment he had second thoughts about his code of honor. He saw immediately that a hero's lot wasn't all it was cracked up to be.

"I'm not taking your bed," she said once they were inside. "The couch."

"Okay," David agreed. "You win one. Lock the door, and I'll be back in a flash." He disappeared, with more jauntiness than he suspected he had left in him, to the bedroom.

Angelina really was tired, as well as being scared.

Maybe it was because the earlier part of the night had been such a fairy tale of wondrous events, that the break-in seemed worse to her than had any other of the myriad dangerous encounters experienced during her life. Or perhaps, she considered as she sat slumped in a corner of David's red leather sofa, experiences were cumulative in their effect.

A person might have a saturation point of fighting off the world. Zoltan had said that the knife of a Gypsy grows sharper from use. But she now had her own the-ory: the knife grows more blunt, and one day the knife crumbles in your fingers when you go to protect yourself.

David returned, humming something.

"I can't believe it," she said, and found a smile forming on her lips. There was something about him, something attractive in the contrast between the mussed hair and the shadow of stubble forming on his cheeks, and the stark formality of the tuxedo. "You're singing?"

David stopped, surprised himself. "I am. Could I be happy?"

"It's almost four in the morning and you and I might have been attacked and maybe killed, and you're singing. That is not happy. That is crazy. You're incredible!" she said, and this time laughed outright. Once unleashed, she couldn't stop the hilarity. When she finally did, she looked through the tears of her hysteria to see David quietly watching her. "What's the matter?" she asked, sniffing and wiping at her eyes as she tried to submerge another round of inappropriate giggles. "You don't look happy anymore."

"Nothing," David said, but to Angelina his expression said otherwise. He started forward quickly, bringing the blanket and pillow to where she sat on the sofa.

"Yes, there is," Angelina objected. "I wasn't laughing at you, not really," she said. "I was just—"

"Angelina..." David stopped. Softly he said, "You're beautiful."

That was all, then he went about unfolding the blanket and stuffing the pillow in the corner of the sofa. "Your new residence is ready," he declared, moving back to admire his work.

The two of them were quiet for a moment, suspended in that strange unnatural silence that occurs when something should be said, but can't be. Anything said would either be too much or not enough.

"I know you hate this," David said, standing by the sofa's side and looking down at her. "You can argue with me tomorrow morning about how I tricked you and used you and abused you. But it's too late now." He had gotten to his bedroom door when he turned and said, "Angelina, you're safe here. From everything." Angelina nodded. "Good night."

"Night . . ." she answered.

She thought sleep would be quick in coming. But it wasn't. She lay against the pillow, seeing David's face against the screen of her mind.

In his room, David stood by his dresser looking down at the frozen, smiling images of his family. The photograph had been taken two summers before, in front of the family estate. A similar shot had appeared in a spread of a national magazine. It was one of the few times David had been exposed publicly to the scrutiny of the mass media. There was always the concern for his safety. The financial power and social prestige of his family both put him in harm's way and shielded him from danger. Always fame and fortune carried a double-edged sword. Soon enough now, his face would join those of his brothers in the national and international spreadsheets. Like those Winthrops before him, and those who would come later, he was programmed to follow the Winthrop star on its course.

But what of Angelina Zarsuela? Would she be protected, as he was? Would her star someday, one day, lead her into a darkened apartment where a stranger waited?

David turned away from the photograph and stared at the door. A few feet beyond, she lay sleeping in his house, safe for the moment.

The thought that at some other time he would not be around to protect her drew him across the room to the door. For a moment he stood with his hand on the handle, uncertain; then unable to resist the impulse to go to her, he slowly turned the knob and opened the door.

Angelina heard the sound and turned her head.

"David?" Her voice was small in the dark.

"You're awake?" He stood only inches within the living room. Outside, below, a cat or a drunk disrupted the lid of a trashcan. A momentary clatter filled the room. "Just wanted to see if you're okay."

"I'm okay."

"I'm not," David said. "Questions keep running through my mind. Like, who that was tonight?" He paused. "And who are you really, Angelina Zarsuela? Where did you come from?" He was speaking rapidly, questions that had barely surfaced in his own consciousness spilling out. "You fight like you were raised in the streets, and you dance like an angel. You're soft as silk and hard as metal. The only man who showed up tonight for you was Guido and the girl I suppose was his daughter. What, were you hatched full-grown a year ago? This was a big night for you. Where the hell were your friends and family?"

"What difference does it make? Any of it?" She felt as if a weight was suddenly crushing her chest.

"I don't know. But somehow it just does. I started thinking in there."

"It's no concern of anyone's, my life."

"I'd just like to know, okay?"

"And I don't know why you are making such a big deal about this! It's four o'clock in the morning!" She was almost yelling. He remained a motionless silhouette in the fuzzy dark, in control of himself as usual.

"You've got some dark secret to hide?"

"No. I have no secrets. My life is an open book. A boring open book. Lots of white pages, okay? I'm Angelina Zarsuela. I live next door. I dance. I have people climb in and out of my window. That's about it."

"No, it's not," David said slowly. "There's more, much more."

"David?" Angelina said. She had raised herself up on her elbows and stared at him through the darkness. His eyes glittered in the filtered street light coming through the drawn drapes. She could see the edges of his face in three-quarter view. It was a handsome face, a face that had known little or no hardship. There were no deep creases, no jagged lines of sorrow or squint lines of cunning, as in the males of her people. "There's really nothing to know about me."

"Angelina," David said wearily, using her same tone, "I don't believe you. Just so you know. It doesn't wash." He waited a beat. "You're right, it's too late for all this now. Sleep well. I'll see you in the morning."

He left her alone again. For the time being she was safe—safe from the past as well as from her intruder.

The sound of a clock ticking invaded her consciousness. Delicate and refined, its well-bred monotony pervaded the atmosphere. Her senses took in the faint aroma of leather and books and the rich earthy smell of a giant potted fern. The scent of security and stability was all around her. For a moment a scene flashed through her mind of what it might be like to be a part of such a setting. She imagined what it might feel like to belong to something lasting and solid and real. She imagined what it might be like to walk across the room and open David Winthrop's door and climb into his bed to offer herself.

A sudden and almost overwhelming heat filled her as she accepted the image of their bodies linked together, moving in the natural rhythm of male and female desire.

The exhaustive demands of dancing did much to keep her mind off physical wants; but there was still a deep stirring that made some nights more impossible than others to sleep alone. This night, thank God, was almost over.

Another woman in her place could have gone to David. This was the modern age of female liberation; or so the magazines said. It would not have been so rare, so strange, so unforgivable. But she could not. She was unfortunately, rare and strange. She was a Gypsy. She did not believe the old hocus-pocus of her clan that only ill fate would follow a Gypsy woman who joined with other than her kind. But she knew through personal experience that trouble had always followed her, and to make love for her was to fall in love. How could she fall in love? Love could only equal doom.

Chapter Five

There was a strange silence between them the next morning. It was as if everything that had transpired the night before, from their confrontive meeting at the party to the incident with the intruder, to David's invasive questions into her past, had not actually taken place.

Reality was now the smell of bacon and eggs and freshly brewed coffee and David sitting across the small dining table in his living room. Through the window, a patch of winter sunlight fell upon his hair, creating a honeyed halo about his face.

With an inner shame, Angelina wondered what things might have been like between them had she given in to her body's appetite and gone to him in the night. She shifted self-consciously in her seat. Before breakfast, she had showered and changed into her favorite all-purpose red sweater and a pair of tight faded jeans.

Now the material seemed to cling to her, making her aware of her body.

Plus, the serene sense of normal domesticity troubled Angelina. Things—her life, to be specific—seemed increasingly to be out of her control. Events and people seemed to happen and appear on their own, sweeping her along in a tide of new encounters. That everything—but for the unsettling experience in her apartment—was beneficent, did nothing to allay the sense of discomfort she still experienced. Life, this new life, good as it was, was unfamiliar. Trouble and strife, those were old friends. She knew their faces well. But having coffee and toast across from a man who had no reason to hide from the police, a man who had not made a boorish attempt to use her body for his pleasure without thought of her feelings . . . well, these were unsettling improvements on the past. Change was disorienting, in and of itself.

"I know you don't like personal questions," David said, passing her a jar of strawberry preserves. "However, we've already spoken of the weather and we've looked at the latest crop of national and international disasters on the paper's front page, you've complimented me on my culinary skills . . . and I'm curious. Have you always wanted to be a dancer?"

"Almost always." Her pulse increased. One answer could lead to more questions.

She realized she must have spoken sharply because David was silent for a moment. He didn't deserve her bad humor. She was about to dredge up some sort of apology when he said, "Well, you're astounding on the stage. I guess you know that." He looked at her, and Angelina fidgeted under the gaze, feeling as if he were seeing more than her face. She had a lot to hide. A whole past lifetime to keep secreted away. "You *will* be famous," he asserted. "Is that what you want? To be famous, Angelina?"

With her fork, Angelina played with what was left of her scrambled eggs as she tried to come up with an answer that would satisfy them both. In fact, she had never really given the premise of achieving actual fame that much consideration. Her mind had more or less run down the avenue that promised respectability. Ballet was strenuous and required physical and mental devotion. There was no time to think of any past traumas or present ugliness—nor of her body's cravings. And then, on stage, in the flood of pink lighting, dressed in feathers or gauze or silk, she could seek refuge in an entire world of total beauty. But she had never thought of fame, as such.

"I do it for the feeling," Angelina explained at last. "When I dance, I forget myself. I get caught up in the music. My body feels, well, like it becomes a part of each note. Every beat becomes a part of me. I love to dance, that's all." She paused, troubled, and searched for the thought that eluded her. Hesitantly she went on, as if the words were being printed out slowly, one by one, in her mind. "I love the feeling of . . . of . . . love." She looked up, surprised by her own revelation.

"That's the only way you can feel love?" David took a bite into a piece of toast. "When you dance?" he asked between chews.

"No, of course not." *Of course, so.* Yes, yes, and yes. And what was worse, she knew he sensed it was true. She felt as if he had just exposed a terrible disease she was hiding, something disgusting. She felt odd and she hated feeling odd in a social sense. She wanted to be like everyone else. "What do you think? I'm some sort of freak? Like I don't have feelings?'' The words ran together in a torrent, angry and sharp. ''I'm sorry,'' she said, wanting to make amends.

''No, I apologize,'' David interrupted. ''It wasn't the sort of thing someone says to a...stranger.'' David rose and began to clear the plates from the table.

Angelina sat where she was, feeling close to wretched and wondering why she should care so much about what he thought or felt. He wasn't anything to her and she wasn't anything to him. And that was the way it was going to stay. She felt as if they were having some sort of a lovers' quarrel. He had chosen the word ''strangers'' purposely to put the relationship at a distance. Still, a full-out cold war wasn't exactly what she had in mind.

Instinctively she knew peace could only be brought about by offering something genuine from herself. It wasn't an easy gift to give. But he had, in fact, risked his life for her. Going back to the original topic, she chose the words of her disclosure carefully. ''I never had much room in my life for love.''

''I didn't know love takes much room,'' David said. He was standing close to her, having brought back a tray to carry the rest of the table setting to the kitchen.

The close proximity to him was unsettling to Angelina. She could smell soap and male cologne. Her eyes fell upon his hands. One hand rested flat against the edge of the tray, the other gathered silver. Tiny golden hairs glistened against the darker color of his skin, which still held the barest trace of summer's radiance. An impression of luxuriant sensuousness filled her as she thought of what the feel of those hands on her body would be like if they lay together on some sun-drenched beach on the Costa del Sol. She would have liked to have reached forward then, to take that hand and hold it against her breast. At that moment she would not have minded if there could be a legal time-out from the life she had fashioned for herself, so she could impetuously give in to her hunger to make love without future consequence.

David's wrist knocked against a glass, and Angelina reached out and caught it before it fell. Her reflexes were those of a born thief; that, at least, was what Zoltan used to proudly proclaim. To think that once she had even held such praise in esteem.

The thoughts were heavy, and Angelina was almost glad to return back to the conversation. "Well, maybe I mean time. There might have been the room for love, but everything was so frantic, it got displaced. We—my family—always moved around so much." *One step ahead of the law,* Angelina mused. "I never thought it was a good idea to become too attached to anyone romantically because, you know, I'd always be going on sooner or later."

David was methodically placing dishes on the tray. Absently, Angelina began to help. She picked up the salt and pepper shakers and wiped off any stickiness with her napkin.

"And what line of work was your family in that kept them on the go so much? Military? Diplomatic?"

"Various occupations," Angelina said, and looked out the window, as if she wanted to escape through the panes of glass rather than continue. "At various times."

David gave her a sharp glance, like a prosecutor, Angelina felt, narrowing in on the telling evidence. "Such as?" he asked.

"Transportation," Angelina replied vaguely. "Why don't you let me help with those?" She rose and attempted to take the tray from him. He held tight to his edge. They were very close and she imagined that he was peering into her mind again, trying to root out answers. If she didn't give him something, he'd just persist and then there would be a fight, and she really didn't want to start another day out with negativity. There was a performance to dance that night. The order of the day was for calm to prevail.

"International commerce, actually," she said, throwing him a lean bone. "My family's large...close-knit. Their enterprises are rather complicated. They mesh with one another, so it's hard to tell sometimes exactly what's always going on." There. She had even generously added some meat.

"What *is* going on?" David asked conversationally, not willing, she could tell, to be politely satisfied with her offering.

"I don't know," she said with pique. "I just told you I don't know what my family does, not really. I don't have a lot of contact with them."

"But you're so close-knit," he reminded.

"They're very...clannish. Not me." He was trying to trap her.

"Why not you?"

He would not stop hammering away on her! "What are you, anyway? A spy? A detective?"

Suddenly he was holding her hand in his and was prying it open. She started to jerk it away, but when she looked down, she saw that he was pulling away a shredded napkin.

"Angelina..." David said. "Look, I'm sorry. I didn't mean to upset you. I only wanted to know about you."

Angelina turned from him, humiliated. She had been giving herself away, all along, and hadn't even known it. Her famous cleverness had deserted her this time. "Oh, God..." She sighed. "I guess I'm tired. I hardly know what I'm doing."

"Look," David said, placing his hand lightly upon her shoulder, "this has nothing to do with being tired. It's got something to do with something else entirely. I don't know what. But I guess I've figured out you don't want to talk about it. I respect that, okay? I'm not going to bug you anymore. But there's just one thing I'd really like from you."

"What?" she asked, turning her face slightly toward him, even as she wished that she could disappear off the face of the earth.

"Honesty. You don't have to answer my questions, but if you do, then be straight with me. That's all. Agreed?"

Angelina closed her eyes. She could not lie outright to anyone. It was against her *own* code of honor. The Gypsy code, such as it was, held that honor was never, under any circumstances, to tell anything factual to anyone, unless they were a part of the family—and then sometimes that was even negotiable.

"What if," Angelina dissembled, "I were to poke and pry into your life, into your things?" She moved quickly away and strolled the apartment, picking up things. "For instance, this?"

She had stopped by a glass table by an arm chair. On it was the clock she had heard during the night. It was gold and housed in a crystal dome. Standing by it, she listened to its voice a moment, admiring its delicate timbre for a second time. "This is beautiful," she said. "No, it's more than beautiful. It's magnificent." And then she added, "And very valuable, isn't it?"

David was impressed. There were many showier items in the apartment if a person was consciously attuned to the finer points of consumerism. But she had picked the most important item he owned. In fact, the clock was a museum piece. It's actual value could not be calculated in dollars, although he was certain it would fetch a handsome sum on the open market if it were ever offered for sale, which it would not be.

"Yes," David answered, "I suppose it is." He suddenly felt uncomfortable. The proverbial shoe was on the other foot now. Personal questions about his family were generally a taboo topic.

The truth was, he did not like to bring up the subject of his family to those who did not already know he was a Winthrop. In the past, such disclosure had had a suffocating effect on any budding relationship. It wasn't that he went out of his way to hide himself; he used his family name openly. Yet he didn't find it in his best interests to flaunt his background, either. People of his "class" automatically accepted him as one of their own, and those friendships—some good, some mediocre, and others putrid—developed in a normal fashion, unburdened by the family's celebrity status.

But other people, once discovering he and the Kennedy children and the Rockefellers and the Getty heirs played on one another's front lawns as equals, either fawned over him or grew apart. Once the connection was made to his heritage, artificiality froze whatever genuine warmth had developed up to that time.

On the other hand, in this particular instance, how could he justify his slip-and-slide avoidance method of social intercourse with Angelina? He had just pried into her own life's history, not to mention the speech on honesty. Bad timing on his part.

With misgiving, he bowed to his sense of integrity. "The clock used to belong to a very famous man. Thomas Jefferson."

"You're kidding? Really?" Looking back at David, Angelina laughed in delight. "A United States president..."

"It was in my family for generations. Periodically it gets passed down when one of us bites the dust. Typically, there's a very large, and deadly boring, coming of age ceremony attended by a lot of deadly boring relatives and friends of the family."

"Okay, I admit it. I'm impressed," she said, examining the clock through the glass case more closely. "I hope you're an only child. Otherwise, your life might be in jeopardy."

David laughed. "I'm safe, thank God. My three brothers each have clocks or watches belonging to other presidents."

"May I hold it?" she asked with a note of reverence.

David thought first to refuse. The clock had only been removed from its case twice before: when it was passed down to him and once when something appeared to be wrong with the mechanism and it needed to be cleaned. He supposed there would be other times in the future when an occasion would warrant the clock's removal. But this request hardly constituted such an event.

He was about to express his regrets when Angelina said, "I've never seen anything so exquisite! I've never touched anything so beautiful and important before. It's like a dream."

And suddenly David was overwhelmed by *her* beauty. And suddenly he felt that he was unable to resist the innocent sincerity of her request. He doubted, as he moved closer to her, that he could refuse her the moon had she asked for it.

"We'll have to be very careful with it," David cautioned as he took his place beside her. Then, frowning he said, "God, Angelina, I'm sorry. I'd completely forgot. I don't know how to open the damn thing. Look," he said, and lifted the clock high to examine its underside. "It's got this devilishly tricky locking mechanism under it. It takes a master locksmith to spring the thing. The glass itself is supposed to be virtually unbreakable. It just looks fragile." *Like you, my lovely dark-eyed, raven-haired neighbor. Like you.*

Angelina, he noted, appeared undaunted by his announcement. She was looking beneath the housing and tracing the locking apparatus with her index finger. Suddenly she stood up, and in a tone of certainty said, "No problem. All it takes is a hairpin, a twist and turn, and *voilà!* we're in and it's out."

And, amazingly, she was true to her word. After one disappointing try, Angelina had liberated the clock. Reverently, she held it in her hand, seeming to derive some sort of spiritual sustenance in being able to hold it.

David watched, intrigued by her fascination over his possession. The eyes, which were so dark as to appear almost black, shone as brightly as the golden clock she was examining. Her entire face was so radiant, like a child who has not yet learned to hide delight. The pleasure she experienced was contagious. It filled him with a happiness he had not felt since his youth.

Impulsively, he made his offer. "Our home—my parents' home," he qualified, "is filled with antiques and objects of art that hold all kinds of legends and mystique. I'm going tomorrow. If you'd like to come, we could drive into Westport together and you'd be able to spend an entire day in what I guess would be considered a collector's idea of heaven."

"Westport? Isn't that where the air's fresh and the grass is green?"

"And the blood is blue—exactly. Westport."

"Do I need a visa from the land of cement to get in?"

"Just your smile at the kingdom's gates will do."

Angelina smiled, practicing, clowning for him. And he could only stand transfixed, the way he had sat in the audience the previous night, captured by her remarkable beauty and the sense of life flowing from her as she deftly proceeded to replace the clock in its safe case.

Her long hair had fallen over one shoulder and without thinking, David reached forward and gathered what felt like a thick stream of silk in his hand. The smile faded from Angelina's lips as she looked up questioningly.

"David . . . ?"

His hand was trembling, he had to drop it to his side. Afraid of what he might do next, he stepped back from her.

"I'd better go," Angelina said. Her face had grown pale. But she didn't move.

David didn't know what to do. He sensed that he was supposed to say or do something, but couldn't be certain what it could be. Anything seemed too much; nothing seemed too little. What little he had with her he didn't want to jeopardize by a false move. "I'll see you tomorrow, then. Would nine o'clock be too early to leave?" His voice was unusually stiff.

"No, no, that's fine," Angelina said as she moved about the room gathering together her things. "I'll be home early tonight. No party for me." Then suddenly she stopped and, looking straight at him, said, "David . . . I can't get involved."

Neither of them moved, nor spoke. Finally he said, "Okay," with a shrug and a light smile, so totally cool, even as he burned inside. Then, desperate, and unable to hide it, his composure crumbled. "Why?"

"I can't. It's my work. I've worked so hard to get to where I am. I can't take any time for . . . you know . . ."

"For anyone."

"I hope you understand."

"I'll see you tomorrow, Angelina."

Angelina shut the door after herself and stood in the empty hall, suitcase in hand. Her eyes were so dry they stung. Her entire being was dry. She felt parched, her soul paper thin and in danger of turning to dust should the slightest breath of life touch it. The handle of the suitcase began to feel molten to the touch. She felt the impulse to flee from the building and run off from the responsibilities of dealing with a heart that would not leave her in peace. She had fought so hard for so long for this dream, and now she found that a new battle loomed larger than anything else in her life. The formidable foe was herself. She was prey to her own emotions. There was no chance that she could have a relationship and come out of it uncharred. And yet the pull toward living life as a real, ordinary, totally complete woman was almost too compelling for her to understand.

When she entered her apartment the contrast with David's made it seem colder and more barren than it had appeared before. She sat down on her bed, staring around the room. Why now, after she had worked so hard and gotten what she wanted, did she seem more dissatisfied than ever before? She had thought she would finally be filled up by all her accomplishments. Instead, she was hollow.

Chapter Six

The long golden box containing the two dozen long-stemmed red roses was on her makeup table after the performance. Many of the other girls in the *corps de ballet* had received flowers the night before. Only Angelina and two others could claim this distinction on Saturday night. Several pairs of curious eyes turned to her as she undid the ribbon. It was never out of the realm of possibility that one of them might—as in the movies and romance novels—attract a stray Prince Charming out of the bodies in the audience. At first sight of the roses, one of the girls sighed and faked a dramatic swoon into her chair. "It's got to be love."

As for Angelina, she at first thought the flowers were again from Guido. Calculating with dismay the expense of such a lavish bouquet, she shook her head as she opened the card that accompanied the flowers.

Your golden opportunity is at hand. Dance, ballerina, dance.

That was all the card said. There was no signature,
only the cryptic message written in a rather childish
scrawl that Angelina knew at first glance did not belong to Guido Rufio. She scowled.

When the girl beside her asked what was wrong, Angelina replied crossly, "I don't know who sent these."

"An admirer, obviously."

"So why isn't there a name?"

"Maybe he's shy? Or maybe he figures you'd know
who it is without signing anything. I don't see what the
big deal is."

"I don't know," Angelina said glumly. "I just like
things to be out in the open."

"Don't worry about it. Roses like that cost an arm
and a leg. You'll be hearing from whoever it is soon
enough. That constitutes a major investment in a relationship. He'll step up to get his pound of flesh, so to
speak, soon enough."

When half an hour later, Angelina exited the stage
door, someone unexpected did, in fact, step up. She
laughed with relief when David Winthrop grabbed her
arm and said, "I was sitting at home, reading my moldy
old documents, when it suddenly occurred to me that
you were far too beautiful to be left on your own after
a hard night's dancing. You didn't eat, did you? That's
what I thought," he answered for her. "So we'll get a
light bite and then I'll see you home safely."

Angelina had no opportunity to protest his enthusiastic plan, and the roses, which she had initially meant
to thank him for, were temporarily forgotten as he rattled on about several different topics simultaneously.

David swept her through the crowd waiting outside the stage door and into a reserved taxi. He continued to talk nonstop the entire time. "I've called my parents and everything's set for tomorrow. They're having one of their social things, so there'll be enough other bodies there for us to get lost and not be too bored. I hope you like lamb. As far as dress goes, everyone will be conservative. So I suggest you wear something startling. Try that black and gold net dress from the show. That would give them something to talk about besides each other. I'm really glad you're coming, Angelina. Truly."

And so it went as they drove down Fifth Avenue.

"Wait!" she managed once. Laughing, she looked him in the eye and said, "Do you think if you talk long and fast and hard enough about tomorrow, I won't say no to tonight?"

David's face took on a look of pleasure and sheepishness, as if he were glad she cared enough to discover his motive, and felt silly because he was acting like any insecure suitor. "Look, I haven't forgotten what you told me, the noninvolvement bit. I just thought I'd overlook it for tonight. And yes, what you suggested, throwing you off guard with my spiel, that was, in fact, my very plan. Apparently it failed."

"No, it didn't. I'm glad about tonight, I want to go."

"You do?" He seemed dumbfounded. "Forgive the surprise. It's just that you're not generally so accommodating."

"I'm not generally so hungry," Angelina returned, afraid of the warmth between them.

"Ah, and I thought that perhaps the acquiescence had to do with my company."

He was fishing, and they both knew it. Angelina turned and looked out the window. She had that feeling again, of life spiriting her away. Things had to be slowed down before everything got out of hand.

"David, there's no sense in believing—"

"No," he interjected. He quickly put his hand on hers, as if doing so would silence words that he did not want to hear.

Just as well, she thought. It wasn't the right moment for a long speech, anyway. She let the matter pass, to be taken up at some later, more appropriate, time that evening.

The "light snack" David had promised was taken at The Tavern on the Green, in Central Park. Angelina was enchanted. With its Christmas decorations up, it was a fairyland of twinkling white lights. Other diners, in their holiday finery, resembled high-spirited sugar-plum fairies. Even the waiters seemed inordinately energized by the spirit of the season. With silent satisfaction, Angelina took in every detail. What a far cry from her tawdry beginnings, where a Christmas might have been spent in a rented hotel room or a battered trailer. There had been good years, too, but generally the holidays were hurtful times for her. The differences between the ways of her family were even more pronounced when passing by windows where gaily lit Christmas trees were displayed in homes where people lived for years and years, and the smells of baking wafted into the streets.

"I thought you'd like it," David said after dessert, interpreting her expression of approval. His eyes glistened back with his own sense of pleasure.

"I do, oh, I really do, David."

"Good," he said, and summoned a waiter for the check. "And it's not over yet."

Ten minutes later, Angelina sat nestled in the seat of a black horse-drawn coach, complete with a formally liveried driver in red cape and high black hat. Flat circles of iced fluff floated from the heavens, dancing around them as they clip-clopped through the streets of New York City. Angelina was only dimly aware of the pedestrians and other vehicles. A bubble of happiness seemed to surround the part of the world she and David currently inhabited.

"I've never been so happy," she sighed in contentment. "It's magic. Real magic. I never knew that life could be so good." Without her realizing it, tears had come to her eyes. "Everything is so good now. I used to dream..."

David had been listening to her, listening raptly to each word. But more so, he was watching her face. Delicate and expressive, he read the proof of her words in the joy mirrored on her face; yet, beneath the joy was a stream of sadness he had not yet found the means to plumb. Although physically near her, he realized he was in almost all ways no better acquainted with her than he had been on the first day their paths had crossed in the Deli Italia. A confusing array of thoughts coursed through his mind as he tried to sort out what it was he really felt for the young woman seated beside him.

Certainly he could categorize part of the attraction under the heading of pure and simple lust. There was also the challenge of the woman. There was a mystique about her, a haunting quality that made him doubt sometimes if she was entirely real. Now and again he would be pricked with a sense of unease, and realize that it was brought on by the insecure notion that she might suddenly vaporize into thin air and be gone out of his life. Her presence—slight and casual as it had been—had certainly energized his existence. His life had not been bad before, not bad at all; in fact it had been rather pleasant. But in contrast with what it was now, her departure from his life would make a wasteland of his emotions. From an oasis of feeling to a dry desert of daily existence: if she left, that was how it would be.

"And, oh . . . I didn't thank you for the roses! They were beautiful, David. I put them in water in my dressing room. Everyone was enormously envious."

At her words, embarrassment and jealousy reared at once, a two-headed beast, ripping through David's composure. *Roses! He had sent no roses!* For a moment, the idea that there was some other male in hot and randy pursuit of his woman, *his woman*, made him almost physically sick. He wanted to do some terrible violence to the bastard. He probably would have if the cretin had stepped into his presence at that moment. Instead, faced only with Angelina in his company, he said a bit too stiffly, "Sorry. You'll have to show your gratitude to someone else."

For a moment, Angelina looked puzzled.

"It was someone else," he explained in a voice of dry anger, as if she were responsible for his outrage. "Not me." As upset as he was feeling, he still couldn't help but notice she appeared even more so. "You don't have to be embarrassed. Wasn't there a card?"

"No. Yes, a card. But it wasn't signed. It only said . . ." She broke off. Out of long habit, she did not share personal information, lest it be turned against her at some later date.

"What?"

"Nothing. It didn't say anything, really. Just some nonsense. It's not important." They were trotting faster now and the snow flew more thickly around them. A fur covering was part of the ride's package, and Angelina pulled it higher and more tightly around her, but, even so, the chill within her did not diminish.

Silence rode like a passenger between them for a few blocks. With every inch they covered, raw emotion churned in the pit of David's stomach. He felt there was nothing to do to reach her. It was bad enough before, with just that infernal barrier she had erected between herself and the world. But now there was the new wedge created by the damnable Rose-Giver. Added to the bleak picture was now a living, breathing competitor. What if this other man were better than he? That, and the thought that there was something lacking in him that made it impossible to breech the inner walls separating them, drove him wild.

Temporarily out of control, he reacted to biological impulse and in one fluid movement grabbed Angelina about the shoulders. He was bigger and stronger and he wanted her and he would take her. Pushing his body and mouth against hers, he closed the physical distance keeping her from him.

Her reaction at first was to struggle, then to offer less resistance when his passion did not subside at the first show of protest; and finally, amazingly, he found Angelina responding with a growing intensity.

At the first touch of his lips against hers, Angelina was surprised; then almost immediately fear took hold. The apprehension did not arise out of any idea that she was in danger of being physically violated, but that she might not *want* to end what he had begun.

A rush of heat sent signals of alarm throughout her body. Danger mixed with pleasure. What thoughts she had were straying like colored ribbons floating from her hair into an infinity of sky. All caution was dissipating.

His hands were in her hair, the stroking urgent as his need for her grew with the response she offered.

Her body switched to automatic pilot, and she realized that even last night she had wanted this of him, and that somehow she was as much responsible as he, through her own thoughts and desires, for bringing them together.

His hand had slipped beneath the fur covering and moved to where her breasts strained against the fabric of her jacket. The buttons gave easily and his thumb and forefinger played against the peaks of both nipples.

She felt control dissolving as his tongue dove against hers, telling the story of his body's yearning, and silently she concurred as she twined her body against his, her hips moving in a serpentine sway.

They were in the middle of the city, yet, enflamed and lost in her internal world, she cared nothing of propriety. Her hand beneath the fur blanket felt beyond his leg and touched him. He pulsed beneath her palm. Dizzy and light-headed from the flow of desire rushing through her own loins, she gave a small sound of abandonment. Before she could remove her hand, he brought his palm flat over her fingers and pressed. This time it was David who drew his head back, eyes closed, an expression of pain and ecstasy intermingling as the warmth of her fingers explored.

Bending into her again, David whispered against her ear, ''We're going home.''

Angelina nodded her understanding, consenting to what was inevitable.

In David's bed, the urgency of their desire during the coach ride increased tenfold, until Angelina wondered at their endurance to reach again and again the summit of ecstasy that left them trembling and slick with exertion. Perfume and cologne mingled with sweat and the scent of their bodies' passion. At a slower tempo, the closeness she felt was almost unbearably sweet as David swept his hand along her inner thigh, then cruised the hollow of her stomach and slipped like silk between the mounds of her breasts. His mouth was hot against a nipple and his teeth toyed gently against the peak. Angelina drew out a moan, and arched her pelvis into his bent leg.

"Angelina…" David said, "one more time and I will die."

"I don't care," she said, moving over him.

"Neither do I. It'll be worth it."

It was only in the first light of the dawning day that Angelina, nestled in the crook of David's arms, remembered the roses. A twinge of fear returned to mar her sense of contentment.

"Do you think they can tell?" Angelina asked David. She smiled back across the room at Lydia Winthrop who, along with David Winston Winthrop IV, appeared to eye her with the same hard look one might engage for a work of art of questionable provenance.

Of course, in this case, their doubts had nothing to do with her outward appearance; she knew she was dressed appropriately in a navy blue wool dress with a band of white outlining the square collar. She had even worn a string of cultured pearls, sent to her three birthdays ago by Zoltan, and only trotted out for a rare occasion. She could easily surmise that their true apprehension lay in what they couldn't discern by naked eye.

"That we ravished the hell out of each other's bodies last night? I hope so," David replied, stuffing a cracker coated with Danish cheese into his mouth. "I'm the only one in the family without a reputation. It's high time, don't you think?"

Angelina might have laughed, but didn't. She was far too preoccupied with another more real fear, against which the supposition that David's parents might guess that they were lovers was inconsequential.

"You should have told me," Angelina said accusingly. "It wasn't fair, David."

David turned and faced her. "Does it really make such a big difference to you?"

"That you're part of all this?" Angelina's eyes swept the room. As David had predicted, the Sunday gathering in the Westport mansion included faces usually only seen in the newspapers and glitzy international magazines dedicated to following the social meanderings of the beautiful and the rich and the famous. "Don't you think it should make a difference?"

"No. I'm still the same man you met and—"

"And slept with last night," Angelina finished in a low voice. They had been standing by a lit fireplace in the huge formal living room. Now Angelina turned away from David and those who might see her expression, and faced the mantle. Over it hung what Angelina knew was an original Gainsborough. She didn't even want to think of what its value might be. Which was the point, wasn't it? *It*, the painting, and everything and everyone else in this house was real, the genuine object. And she was a fake. Through and through she was a counterfeit item and someone, given time enough, was bound to discover the deceit.

Oh, yes, for the moment she was safe. She had been well trained by Zoltan. There was no problem today in carrying off a five or six hour command performance.

It was a mere exercise in superficiality, and any Gypsy was accomplished in the art of pretense. Putting on a new disguise of clothes or personality was as simple as breathing in or out. But, there was one requirement. One single, absolutely mandatory requirement that had to be there to support the performance: the actress had to believe in the play. And she did not.

Her heart was not into sleight-of-hand and illusion any longer. Her heart craved the reality of the passion she had shared that night with David. Just feeling his presence near her filled her with a physical and emotional warmth she had never known existed. And this partially opened heart of hers yearned for the sunlight of honesty. She wanted warmth to continue to spread through the dank coldness that had lodged in her for those many years of deception. Fact: the role of David Winthrop's lover called for the genuine article. She was not right for the part.

"You're as good as anyone here," David said. He edged around into her line of vision where she could not ignore him, nor the topic at hand.

He was careful to keep his face placid as he spoke, but his voice had a harder edge to it than Angelina had previously heard. She wondered at this new side of him. Almost from the moment they had arrived at the Winthrop estate his demeanor had altered. At first she had suspected her observation was due primarily to his change in wardrobe. He had shed the easy, casual attire of his Greenwich Village persona for an expensively tailored version of himself. The gray cashmere jacket he wore was nothing chosen off a rack, regardless of the store. His shirt was likewise impeccably tailored with his monogram on pocket and sleeves, and the black pants were immaculately creased, of perfect length, and the finest wool. The shoes would not have been a penny less than nine hundred dollars, and she knew them absolutely, by the leather, the stitching, the design, to be Italian and handmade. A Gypsy's eye was an educated eye, and Zoltan had been a tireless professor. Her degree was in Life, from its bottom to its top.

"Being good has nothing to do with it," Angelina replied. "Being acceptable because I am like you people has everything to do with it. I am not like anyone here."

"Listen to me. The money in this room has come out of centuries of banditry and the kind of luck that's worn thin in this universe today. No one could amass that kind of wealth again. So the circle has widened, Angelina, to include people who—"

"Are amusing? Cute little human beings who have interesting little talents and perform for these people like trained dogs?"

"Sometimes," David conceded.

"Well, good. You're being honest."

"I told you I'd be. I didn't lie, I just indulged myself in omission. So maybe I should have told you who I was, but I didn't because I was afraid of precisely this."

"It's a reality, David, that's why you were afraid of it. You just didn't want to deprive yourself of some temporary entertainment, like the others here. Did it ever occur to you what I might feel after I get discarded?"

Something in his face made her step back. She had thought for a moment that he was going to hit her. And at that moment, she wouldn't have blamed him. Every insecurity she had ever felt had somehow surfaced and twisted into the barbed syllables of nastiness.

"I'm sorry," she said, and touched his arm. "You didn't deserve what I just said. You aren't a user."

Before David could reply the dinner bell sounded, and Lydia Winthrop was suddenly by her side, ushering her into the baronial dining room. Without surprise, Angelina was seated beside David's mother. David was put across from her, and his father took his place at the other end of the huge mahogany table.

"You must tell us more about yourself, my dear," Lydia said in her crisp voice.

To Angelina, the way Lydia spoke sounded like paper being torn in an absolutely straight line. Zoltan would have applauded his daughter's performance that day. She knew it was impeccable, as she began a fiction to please her rapt audience.

"My father's a wine baron—how the media always puts it. As his father was before him, and his before, and—" Angelina waved her hand absently and trilled a laugh as light and affected as that of the most careless debutante "—his father before him. You know... typical family dynasty stuff," she said, and looked about the table in apparent collusion with all others who were so economically blessed, so elevated in social rank.

"Spanish?" asked David Winston Winthrop from his end.

"Yes. Five hundred years ago my family was given the Zarsuela coat of arms."

"And how do they feel about your stage career, dear?"

"Well, of course, they would have preferred I marry right out of finishing school, to someone *right*, but the ballet was . . . a calling, you see?"

Her eyes met David's across the table. He was staring at her curiously, as if he couldn't quite believe what he was seeing and hearing. Angelina nodded and smiled sweetly. *So what?* He put her in this miserable position. He can just jolly well choke on her words.

After the meal, she was rushed around the house on the arm of Lydia, with David following along. He said almost nothing as Lydia showed Angelina the various art collections, china collections, Oriental carpets, and furniture of a quality that belonged in a museum or a castle dedicated to public viewing. Outside of the world's great museums, Angelina had not ever seen so much personal treasure in one single place before. Perhaps to annoy David—who she now decided was furious and punishing her with his silence—she continued with her impersonation of an aristocratic brat. As for Lydia, she seemed to find her charming and was delighted when Angelina knew the names of artists and the styles of furniture and even the value of a rare Chinese vase. Proof positive of her rarefied social origins!

"How the hell did you know all of that?" David asked coldly as they walked to his car that evening. "You sounded like an art dealer."

"I go to the museums. The real ones, not the kind you're accustomed to living in."

"You didn't have to put on that stupid show in there."

"That's easy enough for you to say," Angelina responded as he held the car door open for her. "You of the silver spoon set."

"Your social and economic status doesn't matter to me," David said, and slammed her door shut.

When he was seated beside her, Angelina continued. "Maybe not. Maybe it doesn't make any difference to you, but it certainly does to them. Do you think they'd be so smiley-faced if they knew you met me in a deli where I was beating up on some crook?''

David was silent. He took a long time before he said, ''No. They wouldn't like it.''

Angelina didn't say anything. Somehow it hurt more to hear the truth stated from his own lips, than it did hers. The truth was the truth, any way you cut it; but it just seemed more the truth when someone else agreed.

''Your mother showed me a Ming vase. That's the kind of stuff that belongs in your house. And me? I'm like one of those vases you win at a carnival when you pitch pennies into a goldfish bowl.''

''I thought you were a ballerina?'' David said, looking at her.

''I am. But that's all I am. There's no more to me than what you see up on that stage.''

''Who did I hold last night, then?''

''I don't know,'' Angelina said, and slumped against the car door. She closed her eyes, exhausted. ''I was my own dream,'' she said. ''For a while. But you know, daylight comes eventually, David, and then it's time to wake up.''

''How do you know,'' he asked, ''if this isn't the reality? What if the other is the dream?''

Angelina opened her eyes. ''What?''

David wasn't smiling. ''Unless you give it a try, how do you really know for sure, Angelina?''

Chapter Seven

In the weeks that followed, Angelina *did* accept David's challenge to test her sense of reality against the dream she was living.

Each day she awoke with trepidation: this day would be the day that the balloon would burst. But each day the joy and fun continued, supported by the sense of security that came from being her own person.

And yes, indeed, she was her own person!

Even the papers were full of her. The company's prima ballerina was lately plagued by ulcers, and on several occasions it fell upon Angelina to take over the lead role in three of the ballets performed during the season. Her performance was caught by *The Times*, and other magazines and tabloids followed suit by sending critics to review the "dazzling and beautiful Angelina Zarsuela."

David was thrilled with her success. It had become his obsession to buy up every magazine and newspaper he could get his hands on and appear at her door with scissors and take-home Chinese food so that they might devote an entire evening to hunting down any new publicity.

But it was not only she who was attracting the media's attention. David himself was getting the press's attention now that he had his Ph.D. and was edging into the political arena under his family's guidance.

Christmas day was spent at the Westport estate. For the first time, only the family was there—except for Angelina. However, as an outsider, she was not treated as such by anyone. And that is what made matters worse.

Being accepted as one of them, as something she was not, was becoming intolerable. Half-truths and minor deceptions were piling up faster than the snow drifts surrounding the house.

"Angelina's becoming a legend," David proclaimed proudly during the Christmas dessert of flaming plum pudding.

A legend constructed of fragile material, Angelina thought, acknowledging David's compliment with a radiant smile. At the first breath of truth, the legend would dissolve. And then how happy would these faces be? Not very, she thought.

"And so also will you, my dear," Lydia Winston said to her youngest son. "A legend in your own time." She raised her champagne glass. "Dear? Do you want to do the honors, or...?"

"You like jewels, Lydia. Take the floor," David's father said.

"What is this intrigue?" David demanded good-naturedly. "You've gotten me another set of diamond cuff links, Mother?"

Lydia glanced at her other three sons. Angelina had the distinct impression that she was present at some sanctified rite of passage that all there understood, having earlier crossed identical terrain. Of the four sons present, one was a United States senator, one a state senator, and one was running for congress. Angelina already knew that one of the "boys" would eventually make a bid for the United States presidency. It took no stretch of the imagination to project that the effort expended in this area would yield fruit. Presently two of the brothers were married. David and Carey, who was running in his first congressional race, were still unwed. Only Carey had come without a companion; the others had wives and children in tow.

Now all the eyes of the powerful Winthrop dynasty were turned to David.

"This is your official coming out, David," Lydia began. "The family's organizing an exchange of art between several nations. It's going to be a very special exhibition. Very important, not only for the quality of art to be shown, but—"

"For the good it will do the family," enjoined David's father from his end of the table.

"Yes," Lydia concurred. "If we pull this off—if *you* pull this off—our name will be cloaked in glory."

"And if I don't...?" David smiled, but his eyes held the same seriousness Angelina had noted among the other sons whenever the subject of family interest came up in conversation.

"You know we don't think in terms of 'can't' and 'don't' and 'won't,'" Lydia reminded sternly.

"We might not, but the rest of the world does," David said.

Angelina was surprised. Rarely did anyone in the family disagree with Lydia. Rarely did they disagree with one another, for that matter. The family's belief system seemed as ingrained in them as the ideals espoused by Angelina's family's had been. That the systems of belief were on opposite sides of the coin was an amusing irony to Angelina. The Winthrops held that nothing would go wrong; the Zarsuelas knew that any plan was likely to misfire.

"We don't care what the rest of the world does, David." Lydia's face had lost its serenity. Her features seemed to pinch inward until she resembled an excited rodent.

"Nevertheless, there is a world out there. And things happen in this world that *can* influence our plans. No matter what you like to think."

"That's enough, son. Your mother has something to tell you."

"I think the time for sticking our heads in the sand is past, that's all," David finished, not in the least cowed by his parents' opposition. "Please, carry on with my destiny, Mother."

"The exhibition will travel to the world's major cities, with our name as sponsor. Of course. It's major focus will be the Phoenix Diamond."

David simply stared. Then he said, "Really?"

"Really..." Lydia said.

And Angelina, herself, thought, "Really?" The Phoenix Diamond, called so for its fire, was famous. Hadn't Zoltan himself licked his lips over photographs of the stone torn out of magazines featuring its tumultuous history? The diamond had never left its home in

Istanbul, where it had been housed for more than a thousand years in a specially built mosque by a particularly cruel sultan. The stone's religious and cultural significance all but outweighed its intrinsic worth as a jewel.

"Our Winthrop bank holdings have guaranteed the stone's replacement value, should anything happen to it."

"Which, of course, it won't," David Senior said. His face had grown pink.

"Because you are to see that it doesn't. You're to be the overseer of the entire exhibition, David. Your picture will be everywhere. In this capacity, you will, of course, meet all the right people and they will meet you. You will, in other words, be acting unofficially as a liaison between high-ranking government officials of many nations."

"How clever," David commented.

Indeed, Angelina thought, and endeared herself by saying, at that moment, "Congratulations, David. This is a wonderful opportunity to assist your family in sharing something wonderful with the world."

The rest of them followed suit, each offering their best wishes for the success of his mission. David accepted the congratulations with a quiet reserve.

On the drive home, Angelina inquired, "What would happen if the Phoenix Diamond got stolen?"

"Before or after I slit my wrists?" David asked.

"David, must you do it? It's so much responsibility."

"I was born and bred to responsibility, my love." He didn't sound elated about it.

"But this isn't just any kind of responsibility. This is the Phoenix Diamond, David. God, not only would you have your parents on your case, you'd have all of Turkey breathing down your neck, not to mention whatever religious groups in other countries felt the diamond was a part of their heritage. It's not just the money, David. It could be downright dangerous.''

"Sometimes you don't have a choice. You're born into danger.''

"Yeah, I'll drink to that,'' Angelina mumbled.

On a March morning, six months after David and she had met, Angelina, walking toward the Deli Italia, made an enormous decision. She had been contemplating the subject for some time; ever since the night she and David had made love. She would come clean about her past. Honesty, at last, would prevail in her life—at least in her most intimate relationship. If David wanted to break the horrible news of her origins to his family, that would be up to him.

After all, hadn't she proven herself again and again over the past several months? Her career had taken a meteoric rise when the duties of prima ballerina were officially split between her and the original star of Sasha's company. Some even rumored that Angelina would eventually usurp the lead position in the company altogether. The summer season was being planned, and there were additional hints that Sasha was going to choreograph and produce a whole new ballet. There was much speculation that those who danced the lead roles would attain instant international recognition.

Guido was helping a customer when Angelina arrived. She waited, and when they were finally alone, she said, "Guido, I have something to tell you.''

Guido looked up from a string of sausages. His brow furrowed as he looked down the length of his lean nose at her. "I don't like the way you said that."

"You may not like what I have to say next, either," Angelina replied tentatively, wondering if, after all, this was going to be such a good idea. But she had no choice. She could not go on living a lie with the people she loved. "But you're going to hear it."

Guido waited. Angelina drew in a breath, and spoke in a rush. "I'm a Gypsy, Guido."

"A what?" He stared at her with the same look a man reserved for someone who announces she is a Martian.

"That's what I am. A Gypsy."

"You? Impossible. From Italy I know what Gypsies are. Gypsies are..." He wrinkled his nose as if suddenly assaulted by the odor of a decaying fish. "Ah, this is a joke! Impossible. Gypsies don't live in New York City and work in delicatessens." He stared at her. "You worked for me how long, and you stole nothing. Did you?" he finished a trifle suspiciously.

"No. Nothing. Of course I wouldn't! I'm not like the others—my family. I never was. Only I got stuck with them. And maybe vice versa."

"Well," Guido said darkly, "now that I think of it, you did steal something."

Angelina paled in alarm. She was about to vigorously protest the remark when Guido smiled and said, "My heart, darling, Angelina. It was my heart you stole."

He rushed around the counter, and Angelina threw her arms around his neck. They embraced for a long moment, during which tears fell freely down her cheeks. In telling him, a tremendous burden had lifted.

"That is why I could never place that strange language of yours."

"It's our own tongue."

"Fine, keep it to yourselves," Guido said. "It sounds like chalk on a blackboard."

As she walked home that day, she felt good, truly good as she had maybe never felt during her entire life. And just imagine how wonderful she would feel after sharing the truth with David! She now knew it was exactly the right thing to do.

Not even the grandest wedding could have been planned with such loving attention to detail as Angelina designed the celebration of their sixth month's "anniversary."

Originally David was as enthusiastic as she was about the evening. He would awake in the middle of the night to tell her he had thought of another, even better, way of spending the special day with each other.

Unfortunately, in the interim, his responsibilities in administering the art show had increased tenfold. On the few nights they had to spend together, he was increasingly exhausted and pensive. Finally, taking pity on him, Angelina relieved him of his participation in the plans for their personal extravaganza.

She had hired another horse-drawn coach and, with Guido's help, she had put together a picnic basket of favorite delicacies, along with a bottle of excellent champagne. That was for openers. After that, she and David were to dine in what was a small, and currently most exclusive, restaurant in the city. This was her treat, entirely. She had come a long way from eating hot dogs on corners. An occasional hot dog was still great, but because she wanted it, not because she had no other choice. Being able to choose was the most notable and wonderful change in her life. She could actually pick which wine to drink or which dress to buy. It wasn't that the "things" mattered so terribly to her in and of themselves, it was the freedom of choice they represented that made them so valuable.

The end of the evening was to be the biggest surprise. In a rented silver limousine, they were to be driven to a cottage in the country. It was an hour's drive from the city, but it might have been a world away in terms of the atmosphere. Angelina had found it advertised in the back of a fashionable magazine targeted for socialite women one day when she was in a salon having her hair cut. The blurb read "Story Book Cottage" and the picture beneath bore out the boast. While David had worked one Saturday afternoon, she had taken the train out of the city and met with the leasing agent who drove her to the cottage.

The house, surrounded by an authentic English garden, was set off a country lane. Vines with purple blooms hugged the gray stone walls in which glistening diamond-paned windows were set. Inside was as charming as the exterior. Flowered chintz slipcovers transferred the garden's profusion of color within. Tables were of fine rich woods and gleamed from polish. Flowers, Angelina was told, would be placed in the largest vases. The bedroom was upstairs and had a high and enormous brass bed with a white goosedown comforter. There were fireplaces in all the rooms, and because the nights still became chilly, there was no reason why Angelina could not expect to use them.

It was perfect, totally romantic and absolutely wholesome. That was important to Angelina. She wanted an atmosphere as far removed in association from the sordid confession she was to make as possible.

Of course she took the place. They would have it for the weekend. Its cost was, needless to say, exorbitant. It didn't matter. This night would only come once. The cottage was a graduation present for her, for having stepped out of one life and into a whole new beautiful one.

On the night of the celebration, Angelina was dressed and waiting for David to knock on her door. She was wearing a new dress, a white knit with tiny imitation seed pearls forming designs of flowers. Her hair had been cut shorter and was worn just below shoulder level. Zoltan's gift of the pearls was around her neck, and she had recently saved for a pair of pearl earrings that she wore. It made her feel good to buy herself nice things; it made her feel safe. Beauty confirmed the reality she had, still only tentatively, established for herself.

Twenty minutes after the time when David should have called on her, she decided to hurry him up. The coach would be waiting for them in Central Park.

She knocked several times before he came to the door. The moment she saw his face, she knew. Something had happened, something very bad.

"What?" she asked. "What is it, David?" She closed the door and followed after him, a hard knot already formed and gaining bulk in the pit of her stomach with each step she took.

He stood with his back to her, the usually straight shoulders collapsed inward. She waited, wanting and not wanting to hear what he would tell her. Finally he turned. "Angelina... I'm sorry. Tonight's off."

"David, why?" This couldn't be happening. She wasn't hearing any of this. If she went back outside the door and knocked again, everything would be different. The door would open and David would be standing before her with a smile on his face. He would take her in his arms and they would begin what was to be the best night of their lives. Instead she stood helplessly staring at David's back. Naked in her disappointment, she tried to fight back the hot tears but lost the struggle. "Everything's been planned. What could possibly be so bad, so terrible, that would ruin tonight?"

"This is," David said, and going to the coffee table by the sofa, picked up the newspaper. He held it out to her.

Angelina took it in her hand and glanced down at the front page. There, in bold black captions, was the Winthrop name, and below it two pictures. One was of David's next oldest brother, Carey, looking as personally secure and honorable as the public might expect a man running for congress to appear. The other image splashed across the page was that of a female. Young and beautiful, her bright smile radiated happiness.

Only, Angelina read, she was not happy. Not any more. Because the woman—Pricilla Camp—was dead.

Angelina looked up, her fingers stiff around the paper. "My God, David . . ."

"Indeed," he said, and for the first time since she had arrived, turned to face her fully. His green eyes were shades darker, as if shrouded by a heavy film of misery. "Go on, read it. The whole miserable thing."

"No," Angelina said vehemently. "It's just gossip. Stuff that isn't true and doesn't deserve—"

"It *is* true!" David broke in. "It's absolutely true. All of it. I didn't want to believe it, either. But I was told. My mother told me. And then my brother. He was in shock at first. Wouldn't, or couldn't, accept it. But he's sedated now. I guess he went crazy when it finally hit that the whole thing was real."

Angelina slipped to the sofa and forced herself to skim the print. Carey Winthrop had been dating Pricilla Camp for the past two years. She was a photographers' model and although not among the top ten in her profession in earnings, was generally considered to be among the most sought after faces in her field. Although Carey had dated other women, it was generally accepted by his closest friends that he was in love with her and there had even been talk of late about a marriage. She was, according to her friends, desperately in love with Carey.

The problem came when the Winthrop family—i.e., David's parents—had hired an investigator to examine Pricilla Camp's credentials as a possible daughter-in-law. Such a policy was "business as usual" according to the Winthrop's attorney and spokesman in the issue at hand. There was a great deal of money, not to mention public responsibility, attached to entering the family.

What the check into her past disclosed was not good at all. Two years ago, prior to her liaison with Carey, Pricilla Camp had been the romantic interest of a known underworld crime figure.

Carey had subsequently been ordered by his family to break off the relationship, lest the taint of her background besmirch his career specifically and the Winthrop name in general.

After the break, Pricilla had gone into an emotional and physical decline, which early that morning had culminated in her suicide. A pathetic note had been left for Carey, stating that her life had actually ended on the night he left her. Her deed was merely an administrative act meant to clear space in the world for those who had reason to live.

With trembling hands, Angelina returned the newspaper to the table. Her head swam. Of course there was compassion for the beautiful girl whose smiling countenance was now a grotesque reminder of life's tenuous nature. But there was also another fear, on a directly personal level. What of her own questionable background? How ludicrous of her to have thought she might hide a family of petty thieves under any carpet trod by a family as powerful and astute as the Winthrops! What a fool she had been, entertaining the notion that by disclosing her past, all would be forgiven in light of her heroic honesty.

Meaning it profoundly, she said, "David, I'm so sorry."

David shook his head. "They want me to come to Westport right away. They're afraid the reporters will be after me for more dirt. Of course I'll have to go. Not to run, but because they'll need me."

She wanted to scream at him that she needed him, too! Just like that poor dead girl in the newspaper had needed his brother—a brother who also had to stick by his family. She wanted, at that moment, to blurt out her own horrible, sordid past and be done with it once and for all. To be done with love once and for all. Because love, she was being so cruelly reminded, hurt just as much as it felt good. Why, oh, why, had she been so stupid to have thought things might have worked out any differently for her than they had for Pricilla Camp?

"Yes, you've got to go," she said, the rage and despair thrashing wildly, silently, in the depths of her soul.

David excused himself to go to the bedroom. He mumbled something about packing a few things. When he returned to the living room, he carried a small valise and a jacket.

It was then she first realized that he hadn't yet begun to dress for their gala evening. He still wore his daytime attire of slacks and a blue shirt with a button-down collar, open at the neck. Standing there in her evening finery, she felt foolish, like a leftover Christmas tree in August. The entire day, while she had been living for the moment they would be together again and celebrate their glorious past and wonderful future, he obviously hadn't given her or the evening so much as a thought. Even now she might have been invisible for all the attention he paid her as he took up his keys.

For a moment she was sure he was going to sweep her up and hold her in his arms. In a burst of sudden emotion he would cry out that he needed her and that nothing and no one would ever separate them from each other. He would see her face, sense her disappointment—because of course, in his love for her, he would be perfectly in tune to her feelings—and insist that they follow through with their plans for the evening. "Life is for the living!" he would say, and kiss her passionately.

"It's going to be one hell of a weekend," he said instead, and held the door open for her to follow him into the hall.

"Yes," Angelina agreed as she stepped past him, "it certainly is."

Chapter Eight

She felt completely shut out of his life.

David did not call her that Saturday morning, and although she waited by the telephone until three that afternoon, there was only one call and that was a wrong number. All her friends knew she would not be home. She would be in the country making love, being in love, with the most wonderful man in the world, and together they would be experiencing the most perfect relationship in the world.

Her closest contact with David that day had been through the *New York Times*. There was another article detailing the tragedy appearing on the second page. Angelina read it with the same morbid sense of interest she would have shown her own obituary. In truth, it could just as well have been her picture in the paper. She and Pricilla Camp were sisters beneath the skin. They had both fallen prey to the irresistible Winthrop mystique and paid dearly for their weakness. Outclassed, they had been cast out.

At four o'clock she decided upon a walk. As she left, she thumbed her nose at the telephone, squatting mute and stubborn on the floor. "Go ahead, ring. Ring while I'm gone! See what it's like to be ignored, you miserable plastic wretch." There it was, the depths to which she had sunk: talking to plastic.

Had Pricilla Camp also waited for her own phone to ring?

Angelina walked alone, knocking into people she hardly noticed passing, crossing at red lights and causing tires to screech. Now and then she looked up to see a man and a woman together, smiling, laughing, arms linked, and she felt her heart twist. Passing a jeweler's, she stopped and stared inside. Through the window she saw a young man and woman seated before a glass display case. The salesclerk had spread out a black velvet cloth on which Angelina could make out the flash of a diamond.

As Angelina peered inside, a drop of rain hit her nose, then another and another. Still she watched, and when she finally turned, her tears mingled with the spring rain that had others running for shelter while she, hardly noticing, certainly not caring, only moved resolutely on.

Her apartment seemed even more silent than before when she returned home.

It was six o'clock, a time more quiet than other hours in her neighborhood. She and David had speculated that this was because the Establishment People were out eating and the Other People were still sleeping, building energy for nocturnal escapades to come. Anyway, it was as quiet as a tomb when she took off her jacket and dropped it over a chair. Even the rain had stopped.

For a while she just sat on her bed and observed the mute telephone as if she expected it might, at any second, do some trick. Like her, it served no purpose. Then, on impulse, she suddenly rose off the bed. She lifted the phone off its receiver and dialed the limousine company. "I reserved a car for last night and had to cancel. I'd like the same car tonight. Is that possible?" At first it wasn't and then it was. At least something was working out for her.

The ride to the cottage took a little more than an hour. When the driver pulled up to the cottage it was already dark, but in the illumination from the headlights, even he had to comment on its beauty. "This place doesn't even look real," he said, opening her door.

"It isn't," Angelina replied, staring at the house. "It's just a fantasy."

Inside there were flowers in all the vases, exactly as the agent had promised. Wood was in the fireplaces, ready to be burned. In the refrigerator, champagne was chilling. There were cheeses and crackers and fruit and tins of caviar, smoked oysters, and a bowl with fresh lemons. And more. Much more. In fact, there was everything there that had been planned, except David.

There was one thing she could do there alone: she could get very drunk. And she did.

The next morning she awoke with a raging headache and swollen eyes from a crying jag that she could only dimly recall. Other clues to her night of solitary revelry were the still-smoldering coals in all the fireplaces, the open and hardly touched tins of oysters and caviar, two empty champagne bottles—one whose contents showed

up partially spilled on the kitchen floor—and an un-
signed letter to David, telling him goodbye.

In a haze of physical pain, Angelina read the emotional missive she had penned during the night. Some
of the words were mere blurs of ink, the original meaning dissolved in what had to be either spilled champagne or soppy tears. What she could make out was so
maudlin. It was so childishly romantic. It was so true.

She tore the three pages up and threw the scrawlings
into the fire pit. A minute or two later, a smoldering
coal ate through her tale of sorrow, devouring it in full
while she watched.

And that was that, Angelina mused as she moved
gingerly in the direction of the downstairs bathroom on
a quest for aspirin. There was really nothing left of her
hopes for a future with David.

The hangover she suffered from her Saturday night's
orgy of self-indulgent pity lasted clear through to
Monday morning. She was supposed to make her appearance at the rehearsal hall, but for the first time ever,
phoned in sick.

"You are not with child?" Sasha questioned appre-
hensively.

"You are not crazy, are you?" Angelina returned
dully. It hurt to talk, and even listening wasn't much
better.

"When someone cannot come, they say many things.
A cold. A this. A that. But later it is not cold or this or
that. They do not come, because baby comes."

"I'm not pregnant. I'm dying. My body is dying of
an overdose of French bubbles."

"Ah, yes," Sasha intoned sympathetically. "They
have done this bad thing to many, many peoples, the

French bubbles. But, I have good Russian cure. I suggest you take—"

"Do you have something for despair, Sasha? What do you have for a broken heart?"

"I am Russian," he said, sounding affronted. "We live to suffer. Life is nothing without misery! Enjoy."

"I'm not Russian. I like things to work out. I like it when love works."

"Passion!" Sasha exploded into her eardrum.

Angelina winced. "Aspirin," she moaned.

"You sure it is not baby coming?"

"As sure as I am that there is a man with a hammer inside my head. I'm damned sure of that, Sasha. Damned sure."

At four that afternoon she was still lying in bed, thinking that she might never leave her apartment again, when she heard sounds in the hallway. Her heart, which had lain like a corpse in her chest all day, gave a harsh thump. She held her breath and listened. There was the sound of David's door closing a second later, and then again, the great, overwhelming silence.

It didn't matter that she looked and felt like hell. The sooner she settled things, the better. Slipping into her robe, she left her room and entered the hall. The floor was moving beneath her feet. The walls were all slanted. She had never noticed how ugly the painted walls were.

David answered her knock. He looked surprised to see her.

"I know I look like hell, David. You don't need to gape. I'm only half dead, not completely gone yet. If they gave an Olympic Gold Medal for the worst hangover, I'd have it."

"I'm surprised," he said, following her with his eyes as she passed into his apartment. "I thought you'd still be at rehearsal."

"And you don't look so terrific yourself," she said, standing several feet away. He did look awful. There were deep blue circles beneath his eyes and he hadn't shaved. He had changed into another outfit, but other than that, he looked to be the same tormented wraith who had floated out of his apartment—make that, out of her life—three days before.

"It was pretty awful," David said. "No, it was damn awful." He ran a hand over his face.

Dimly, Angelina felt a warming flow of sympathy creep into the coldness that had taken residence in her over the dismal weekend. Of course it must have been dreadful for him!

But then the newspaper lying on the table caught her eye, and the smiling face of Pricilla Camp absorbed her compassion.

"They were all so upset. Like children, really. The ugliness. They aren't used to dirt touching their lives. I think that somehow they thought it didn't actually exist. They've given away hundreds of thousands of dollars in their time to people who had no money or were dying of something that might have been cured but for lack of money. But I don't think they ever really believed that they were real people who actually suffered."

"Oh," Angelina said coldly. "It must have been quite a shock. Poor things, to have their noses shoved into reality like that. It probably spoiled their weekend."

David looked at her, at first with confusion, then with understanding. "You're angry," he said. "Not at them. At me."

It was her cue. She waited a beat, allowing for a last minute retreat from her purpose. Her resolve wavered. It would be so easy to let the whole thing drop, to continue on with the charade and let the romance play itself out in a natural manner. That was the course most love affairs took, wasn't it? Grand passions turning to great yawns. Maybe she would even be the one to fall out of love. Maybe she would meet someone else one day in Guido's deli and then, instantly, she would know that he was Mr. Right. David would be nothing. He'd fade from her life like the image on an old photograph. Everything would resolve itself. Oh, sure, sure they would; just like elephants would be born with wings.

"David," Angelina said, "over the weekend I had time to think." She paused; there was still time to stop. "And I realized that my career was very important to me. There's really not room for our relationship if I want to take advantage of all the opportunities that—"

David rushed to her and grabbed her with such force she gasped. "What the hell are you saying!" he shouted. He shook her, his eyes flaming. "I've just come back from...and now you...?" He dropped his hold on her and spun around in a circle, as if unsure of his surroundings. When he looked back he said, "The one thing that kept me sane over there was the thought of coming back to you. That you were here for me. That the two of us were so solid and real that no matter what craziness my family—and the whole world—dished out, there would be *us*. And now...shit!...now, Angelina, you're going to tell me your career is more important than—"

"How important is your family to you? Your family is *your* career. At least, David, I had the originality and independence to go out and find something for myself, something that is mine and separate that I love to do. I'm not some emotional puppet!'' She was screaming, *screaming* at him! David was facing her with the look of a man who had no defenses at his disposal. His entire being was exposed to her, and what she saw was an image of herself, the heart open and raw, shredded and bleeding, pulsing with a desperate hope that it would be spared the final, absolute blow.

"Oh, God, David . . .'' she said, and ran the distance between them and fell into his arms. Clinging to him, she cried, "I'm sorry, I'm sorry, I didn't mean to say it. I love you so much I don't know what to do. I feel like dying when I think that I might turn out like that poor woman.''

"Angelina, no . . .'' David said, emotionally ravaged. He lifted her tear-stained face in his hands. "That would never happen to you. How could it?'' he soothed, running his hands through her hair. "I would never leave you, never.''

"Oh, David,'' Angelina choked, "you don't know that. If you found out anything about me—''

"I know you! Inside. Outside. Your mind, your heart, your body, Angelina. What more is there to know than this about a person? And I love you, all of you, and will forever.''

Angelina closed her eyes, and in despair—an even greater, deeper chasm of despair than she had experienced over the weekend—burrowed her body against David's chest and sobbed. For now she knew that she could not tell him. Over the weekend her fear of being rejected had made her brave, but her love—this maddening love—rendered her weak. The lie would continue. And whatever time she would have with him, she would cherish.

"You're not ever going to be in the same place as Pricilla Camp," David said, drawing away and taking the newspaper into the kitchen. Angelina heard him toss it into the garbage. He came back.

"David, you can throw away a paper, but that doesn't change things. Your family is capable of—in fact did— throw away a human being. That's a fact."

"I am *me*, Angelina. In spite of what you think." He spoke softly as he crossed the room to where she waited. "I'm not really some satellite personality. I do what I do because I happen to believe in some of the same things as my family. The members of my family are not infallible, no one is. They do some worthwhile things, and I know they've done some horrendous things. But I can't change who I am. I was born into this family. I was born with the proverbial silver spoon in my mouth. What good is served by walking away from the influence my family's name carries if I can use it to improve the conditions of people less fortunate? I won't turn my back on my family, Angelina. Partly because in spite of their stupidities and arrogance, I love them. And partly because I want to use the power they've stockpiled over the generations. I rest my case."

"Oh, David . . . my love, my dearest, wonderful, noble, love . . . I find you totally innocent!"

They made love in David's large bed. They were both exhausted, but even so, the lovemaking was sweeter and more complete in its fulfillment than Angelina had ever experienced. There was a sense that each not only desired, but cherished the other.

As much as she had held back emotionally from their relationship during the past two days, Angelina gave now. She abandoned herself totally to his embraces. His needs were her own and without shame she found herself responding with an urgency that might have previously embarrassed her. As he slipped down her body, she arched against his mouth, calling out his name, absorbed in the fire of their union.

"I could never live without this," David murmured, his breath hot against her neck. "If you left, I would find you. I would hunt you down...I would take you—" hardened, he slipped within "—like this. Again and again and again, I would have you," he said with every movement, until Angelina cried out from the exquisite pleasure.

Angelina's fingers traced over his body when he had finished and lay still, at last, beside her. His body with its rippling, sinewy muscles, was as smooth to the feel as liquid silk. At her touch, she saw his stomach contract and the instant rush of desire fill him again to readiness. "Not possible," she laughed softly, but it was, and he proved it by bringing her hand to him.

In turn, the knowledge that she could arouse such passionate feelings in him excited her to express her own adoration. The lovemaking was a celebration. Each kiss was a candle being lit within her heart, the glow of light extending throughout her body.

He brought her atop him and looked deeply into her eyes, watching the effects of his explorations reflected in her expression. Angelina closed her eyes, the pleasure intense. "Look at me, love...look at me," David urged, his fingers encircled her waist as he rotated his pelvis beneath her.

Shivering with ecstasy, Angelina moved with him, her body an ocean of heated pleasure.

Bringing her down, his mouth hungrily took in her breasts. Her breathing quickened. A feathery excitement rushed along every nerve ending contained in her body. Slick with perspiration, Angelina pressed into him, arching her back and crying out his name.

David held her tightly. His body was hard, straining against her, the rhythm continuing through the initial ebb of her release. He brought her back again, his control steady, until Angelina gasped, wracked by a second, even more intense round of explosive contractions. Like stars shooting from the center of a galaxy, pinpoints of exquisite delight burst again and again within her.

His lips were hungry against hers, his hands demanding to possess all of her as they coursed over her body. A tempest stirred again in Angelina. Clinging, she rode through another wave, opening herself to the pleasure. "Oh, God, Angelina..." David said in a low animal growl, and turned her beneath him.

She felt him tremble, felt the force of his need as he stiffened, remaining quiet for a moment as he preserved his control for one minute more. Then, slowly, surely, he entered and began his own climb. At the summit, he shuddered, gripping her with the full strength of his body as if he meant to merge body and spirit with her. Hot, his body was a flame searing into her. A flame burning every last vestige of resistance to their love.

Joy filled her, expanding her heart, until Angelina felt she might suddenly lose her senses with the happiness and wonderment of not merely loving, but being loved, herself. She had touched him to his core, and he had entered every secret part of her own self. There was nothing higher, nothing more beautiful.

They had fallen asleep in the dark, cradled in each other's arms. The clock said midnight when Angelina awoke, feeling David stirring beside her.

"Are you awake?" he whispered.

"Now I am," she answered with a laugh.

David slipped his arm from her and, turning, switched on the light beside his bed. The shade's amber canopy cast the room into a wash of serene golden light. Angelina watched, groggy, while David left the bed and moved across the floor to his dresser. In the haze of gold his body hardly appeared real in its perfection. Angelina's breath caught as he turned around and she caught the beauty of the man she loved in its full force.

So moved was she by the sight of him, in his natural and stunning maleness, she paid no attention to the small box he carried back to the bed until he handed it to her.

"I'd meant to give it to you on Friday."

It was a tiny velveteen box. Angelina opened it, wishing she had thought to buy him some trinket, too, but hadn't, due to her preoccupation with the other plans for their "anniversary." But it was not "some trinket" that she viewed in the halo of burnished light. In its bed of silk sparkled a round diamond of such brilliance and fire it seemed to be a living, pulsing presence.

For a moment Angelina merely stared at its beauty; then she raised her eyes slowly, as the implication of the gift seeped through.

"I love you, Angelina. I want to love you forever, for my entire life—for *our* entire lives. Marry me? Marry me, Angelina, so that this—" he lifted his shoulders, opening his arms as if to encompass every beautiful feeling they had shared together "—can go on and on and on. Forever."

"Oh, David..." Her heart beat wildly, and she was so besieged by swirling emotions of every type and intensity she felt she might black out from dizziness. Love and fear, certainty and crippling doubt, reckless abandon and immobilizing caution, all of this tumbled in circles, crazy mental tigers chasing one another's tails. "Yes, yes!" she said, the words bursting from her.

David swept her into his arms. He pressed her against him, tight and hard. His heart was pumping as madly as her own. His love was as mad as her own.

"Forever and ever and ever," David said, kissing her wildly, lips, eyes, ears, neck, devouring her, possessing her.

And Angelina held fast to him, the glory of the moment almost more than she could bear. Such complete joy!

Chapter Nine

The announcement of their engagement was made a week later in all the newspapers. The weekly magazines were already wild to have pictures of Angelina Zarsuela and David Winthrop together. They had dredged their photographic morgues for publicity pictures of both parties. The search proved only marginally worthwhile in the case of David; prints were few and mostly from his childhood. There was nothing exploitive or extravagant available on him. To compensate for the lack of titillating copy on David, there was the expected journey into the recent past, to capitalize on his brother's scandal.

Angelina, however, was an enigma to the press; a state that Angelina intended to preserve. Guido promised that no word of her Gypsy heritage would escape his lips. ''May the Blessed Virgin turn the next ten years of my cash receipts into pickle juice, should I utter a syllable!'' Baffled and miffed that they could turn up not the slightest shred of information on her early history, the press pursued her wherever she went.

They were making her crazy, camping outside of the rehearsal hall—Sasha had barred them from entering—and hounding her through the streets.

"Why don't you just sit down and tell them what they want to know?'' David suggested. "It's not like you're a criminal or anything. The worst they could find is that you're a bore like me who hasn't done anything to excite the public's bloodlust.''

"No!'' Angelina said passionately. She hated these discussions. Both of them knew full well it was David who would like more light shed on her undisclosed personal history. His curiosity and her refusal to satisfy it clung to their relationship like a weight they were constantly dragging behind them, feeling its effects, but never turning to acknowledge the impact it had on their lives.

As the subject arose again this time, they were in his apartment. They had just finished compiling a list of people to invite to the party that would officially announce their engagement. It was to be thrown by the Winthrops at their South Hampton home.

"Anyway,'' Angelina went on, trying to lighten the mood, "mystery's good for my image as a performer. It's tacky to throw yourself at the public. Look what being hard to get did for Garbo. She was only an actress. Now she's a legend.''

"Look, Angelina, *I* don't even know about you,'' David said, addressing the subject directly.

God, she wished he would just leave the matter alone. Hadn't he ever heard of Pandora's box? Angelina cast her eyes down to the neat list she had compiled of friends' names. David followed her gaze and, taking the paper in his hand, held it before her as evidence. "There's no name on this page connected to your past, other than Guido and his daughter. No family. No friends. Not even an old lover. I would have even welcomed a dozen old lovers, Angelina!" In frustration, his voice had risen. Pausing, he said more evenly, "I think I've a right to know something more about you."

Angelina stood and walked to the window. Her back was to him. Looking out at the street, she said, "I don't like to think about the past, David. I haven't done anything wrong. Believe me. As for my family, my father was a businessman. He wasn't very successful. He made a lot of mistakes, as a matter of fact. But he really meant well." At this statement, she turned around and faced him. Her eyes were misty, even as her expression was defiant. "He tried."

"What kind of business did he fail at?" David asked, trying to keep the dialogue going. "Maybe we might help him in some way...through my family's interests. God knows we've helped enough strangers. Why not a relative?"

"No," Angelina said. Her lips turned up slightly. Her mind had displayed an image of her proud, pugnacious father. "My father's not one for accepting charity. For better or worse, he's his own man, He follows his own star." But that was not enough information, and Angelina sighed, knowing that David would still want the other part of his question answered. "He was involved in international trade, mostly." It was not entirely a lie.

"Your father sounds very illusive," David commented dryly.

"Illusive, yes." A Gypsy lived in the cracks of the world, sliding in and out of shadows, dodging the truth as he did the bill collectors.

"I suppose that's where you get it from?"

"I want my life to be private." It was a weak defense. She would move to an offensive position. "What's so wrong about that? Your family's no different. I'm sure there are other skeletons being guarded in your closets besides the thing with Carey and Pricilla. I don't see any need to bring them out and rattle their bones around."

"But if you wanted to see them, I'd open any door for you myself. You're a part of me, Angelina. There's no separation between my life and yours. I had hoped you'd feel the same way."

At his words, a crushing sadness weighed in on her. Yes, he was a part of her; no, the whole of her! But he could not know all there was of Angelina Zarsuela. If he did, he might be repelled. Even if he were not disgusted by her past, he would never have a day's peace for worrying that the press would somehow discover her secret life. For his sake, she had to guard that part of her life. She felt she could do it. After all, there were no leads, no loose threads in her life for the media to follow. Paranoia being second nature to a Gypsy, she had been careful never to socialize in school. And, as far as having lived with her American family—reformed Gypsies—they would never come forward. No Gypsy wanted to be scrutinized too closely. Long and bitter experience had proven to them that even in their innocence they were easy targets to assume the blame for baffling crimes.

"David," she said, not moving, "I would die for you. I would."

With the light from the window behind her, her face was cloaked by shadow. Her large eyes, deep-set normally, were veiled now, not only by the luxuriant fringe of black lashes, but, David thought as he looked across the room at her, by a deep somberness having nothing to do with shadings of light. A twinge of apprehension traveled across his mind. Her mention of death, the mere thought of any separation between them, was too horrible to contemplate.

"I'd rather have you show your love by living for me," he said quickly, to render her statement impotent.

Angelina's expression grew instantly soft. She stepped forward at once, running to him, and in the light that fell upon her face his fear dissolved. Her eyes were clear and bright, and filled with love. He saw it; he felt it streaming into him as he clutched her against him.

The wedding was a month away. It was to be a June bash, a tradition among the Winthrops. Angelina had already expressed her profound regrets that her family would not be able to attend on such short notice. Hating herself, she craftily came up with various excuses for their respective absences, from illness to business involvements.

She mailed the invitations—and on that very day, she received an unexpected visitor. From that moment, all her plans, every glorious thing that was to follow, were instantly changed.

She had returned from the first rehearsal of a new modern ballet, put together for the troupe by Sasha. It was his first try in this style, and everyone loyally worked extra hard to make his vision work. Subsequently, Angelina found herself to be continuously physically exhausted, and at the same time mentally preoccupied with a thousand details related to the elaborate wedding. Her state was such when she walked into her apartment.

She had considered moving several times. Even on her own, she might easily have afforded something far nicer than her current residence. She and David had talked it over, however, and felt the move would be too much trouble for both of them at the present. David's involvement with the art exhibition was deepening with each day, and her own energies were spent rehearsing the new season's dance offerings. The plan was to find a spare day or two before the wedding to search out new digs for their first home. So far the day hadn't turned up in their schedules.

So that evening, when she switched on her wall light by the door, she entered into the familiar space of her old apartment. Sure of her territory, she moved like a sleepwalker from the living side of the room to the small galley kitchen area. Opening the refrigerator, she idly examined its contents for traces of edible food. She hardly felt like taking a trip to the market. If she moved one more muscle her life would be over.

It was then, with the cool of the refrigerator against her face, that she felt another chill against her neck. It was so subtle at first that she dismissed the first sensation as her imagination. However, a second later, as she was contemplating a salad, but wishing for a steak or pasta or a mountain of chocolate, a distinct draft blew against her back. Its force rattled papers lying near the telephone. From the corner of her eye, she caught the edges of note paper straining to be blown free. Satisfied that they were firmly anchored by a coffee cup and several pens, she would have gone back to her surveying when another sound—stealthy, like the scramble of quick, light steps—made her whirl around.

Too late.

A hand clamped over her mouth and, with lightning speed, her head was jerked back. The view of the open window—the window she had closed that morning—passed before her in a blur, the drapes fluttering like hands waving goodbye.

With her heel, she gave a mighty kick to her assailant's shin and at the same time, dug her elbow into his rib cage.

An "oomph" sounded behind her, followed by a curse, and she was whipped around to face her attacker.

Crouched, ready to spring forward in defense, Angelina instead merely gaped, remaining motionless in surprise. When she could finally gather her wits, she said, "You!"

"It appears so." The man stepped lightly away. He moved to the sink, where he helped himself to a glass of water. "That hurt, incidentally."

"Good. I could kill you, Ramon," Angelina muttered between clenched teeth.

"And dance at my funeral, no doubt," he replied evenly. He wiped his mouth across his sleeve and went back for a second glass of water. "You almost did kill me, little sister. I'd forgotten how tough you are. But then we Zarsuelas are a brutal lot, aren't we?"

Angelina eyed her older brother with clear distaste. "Don't lump me in with your kind."

"Our *kind*? Our *kind*, you say?" Ramon left the sink and began to circle her slowly, eyeing her up and down as he did so.

4 FREE Silhouette Desire titles. . .
to gladden your heart and quicken your pulse!

Your introductory gift from Silhouette.

Passionate, sensual, charged with emotion. . . Silhouette Desire brings you all the heart-break and ecstasy of fulfilling contemporary relationships as they are lived today.

And to introduce you to these no-holds barred, exhilarating stories, we'll send you 4 Silhouette Desire titles, and a digital quartz clock, absolutely FREE when you complete and return this card.

We'll also reserve a subscription for you to the Silhouette Reader Service, which means you'll enjoy:

★ SIX WONDERFUL NOVELS — sent direct to you every month.

★ FREE POSTAGE & PACKING — we pay all the extras.

★ FREE REGULAR NEWSLETTER — packed with competitions, author news and much more

★ SPECIAL OFFERS — selected exclusively for our readers.

There's no obligation or commitment — you can cancel your subscription at any time. Simply complete and return this card today to receive your free introductory gift. No Stamp is required.

Free Books Certificate

Dear Jane,

Please send me my 4 FREE books and FREE quartz clock. Please also reserve a special Reader Service Subscription for me. If I decide to subscribe I shall, receive 6 superb new titles each month for just £6.60 post and packing free. If I decide not to subscribe, I shall write to you within 10 days. The free books and clock will be mine to keep in any case.

I understand that I am under no obligation whatsoever — I can cancel or suspend my subscription at any time simply by writing to you. I am over 18 years of age.

6S7SDB

Name: _____
(BLOCK CAPITALS PLEASE)

Address: _____

_____

_____ Postcode _____

_____ Signature _____

To Jane Nicholls
Silhouette Reader Service
FREEPOST
PO Box 236
Croydon
Surrey
CR9 9EL

NO
STAMP
NEEDED

SEND NO MONEY NOW!

Angelina, in her turn, surveyed him. Ramon had always reminded her of a cat, one who strutted and slunk along alleys. He was lithe and tough. His muscles were hard and stringy, no spare fat anywhere on the body that was used as a machine to get him what he wanted. There was also, Angelina recognized with sinking regret, a strong family resemblance between them. His eyes, like her own, were large and so dark as to appear almost black. There was a delicacy of bone structure to his features, as well. The cheekbones were raised and slanted, and slightly exotic looking. A full mouth that could pout appealingly at will, or smile ingratiatingly, even as he picked a pocket, could move fluently through several different languages. Irresistibly attractive to women, he used them with the same fastidious skill he employed in all of his nefarious dealings. It was easy enough to see why women went for Ramon, even why men admired him. Ramon had style; she'd give him that. Now, standing before her in the tacky surroundings, he was dressed in a fine outfit of expensively tailored slacks and a sport shirt with a designer insignia. Of course, they had to be stolen. That went without saying. To Ramon, there was only one real sin, and that was to pay cash for anything.

"You know, Ramon," Angelina said, finally over her initial fright, "you're a clever, clever one. That much I'll give you. But," she said, moving toward him, "sometimes you are too clever for your own good. That's the problem you have. If you would use that busy little brain of yours to do something legal for a change you might actually get somewhere in this world." She looked into his handsome, seemingly concerned face.

"Quite right, little sister. You have just pointed out a condition of my personality, recently noted by myself. And it is one I intend to rectify. I am turning over a new leaf."

"Ha!" Angelina spat, and walked away from him. She looked about the apartment.

"I didn't touch anything this time," he assured her. "Really. Trust me." A brilliant white smile broke over his face.

"Oh, give me a break, Ramon." Then her face clouded and her eyes narrowed. "You...it was you, both those times. You took my money the first time. The second time you—" She started for him, rage filling her.

Ramon backed away, holding his hands out to her in supplication. "Dearest sister...sweet little Angelina...I only borrowed the money. I would have asked, but then you would have said no. And I really did need it. Truly. It's all for a good cause. You will see. It will be returned, of course. And with something added to it. But not quite yet...almost, but not quite yet. But you did like the roses, yes?"

The roses! Of course, the roses. He had been spying on her all along! Playing with her!

Angelina picked up a vase with some dying flowers, leftovers from an admirer from a recent charity performance the troupe had danced. Hurling it at him, the vase exploded against the wall, missing the intended target as he danced around the room like a tricky cat.

"You might have just said thank you. But, ah, violence is always becoming in a woman. Lends an edge to the relationship. You'll make someone a fine, fine wife."

And then Angelina, who was thinking in terms of the iron skillet in her kitchen, froze.

"A fine wife..." Ramon repeated, gathering control over the situation.

They faced each other, brother and sister. Both, so alike in their features, registered the same understanding.

"Yes," Ramon began, and the humor disappeared from his face as quickly and efficiently as a light bulb extinguished by a flick of the finger, "a wedding is an important event. So you see, we must talk seriously, the two of us." He motioned her to sit on the bed.

Heavily, Angelina obeyed, knowing it would be futile to resist. The talk was inevitable. From the bed, she stared across at him. He had brought over a wooden kitchen chair and straddled it, its slatted back to her, his arms relaxed over its top rung.

"You see, little sister, what you say really has a great deal of truth to it. I'm thirty now. Not so old. But, not so young, either. And, it's time I think seriously about my future."

Angelina narrowed her eyes. "I don't see what your future has to do with me, Ramon."

"I think you do—in generalities, anyway. I've given this upcoming alliance of yours a lot of thought," he said, and nodded with the wisdom of a sage. He rose up, invigorated by the vision of the future he was about to disclose. "I am very proud of you, Angelina. You've done something with your life. Something great. And," Ramon added, turning back to Angelina and looking at her with as much warmth and genuine feeling as she had ever seen him display, "I want you to know how much, how very much, I admire you."

Even Angelina had to melt beneath the steady gaze holding such heartfelt goodwill. Nevertheless she was not without caution. "Thank you, Ramon. I'm proud of what I've done, too. It took a lot of work."

"You're going to be rich, Angelina!" He threw up his hands, and spun around like a dizzy top. "Rich!"

"Ramon, I might be well off perhaps, if I make it to the absolute top. But a ballet dancer hardly earns the kind of money that constitutes real wealth." Ramon just stared at her, simply stared.

And in that single look Angelina realized her error. She almost laughed herself. How gullible she was, even she who knew what a sly, ignoble person her brother was. They had been speaking of entirely different things. He was talking of oranges; she of apples. The subject of his visit was singular: her marriage to David.

"I love the man I'm going to marry. Rich or poor, I love him. His money means absolutely nothing and it will not benefit my life in any appreciable way. It will also not benefit *your* life."

"Ah," Ramon said darkly, "but here you are wrong."

Angelina rose from the bed. Pointing to the door, she said, "Get out. And this time use the door."

Ramon ignored her. "You can't turn your back on me," he said firmly. "We're family. You owe me your loyalty. Just as I would be there for you, if you needed me. Oh, I know—you think I'm selfish, a bad penny."

"Nooo," Angelina said, "how could you think such a thing?" She glared at him. "The only person I feel anything for in my family is my father. And *he* would be as sickened by you as I am. All he's ever wanted for us, for all of us, Ramon, is that we lead decent lives. You know how hard Zoltan tried. Again and again and again. And now he's old, and he's made a success of himself. And there you are, ready to thumb your nose at all he's built for us over the years. Legitimacy, Ramon! Think of it. We'll never have to run again, or hide again . . . do you know how good that feels? To walk in the sunlight, and not skulk around in the shadows?''

When she had finished, Ramon waited a moment, considering something. "You're right. And . . . you're wrong." Speaking as seriously as Angelina had ever heard him, Ramon proceeded to tell her where she had erred.

"Our father did have a vision to come clean, so to speak. But it failed."

"Failed? It didn't!" she protested, but the laugh that followed was unsure. "Zoltan's got his vineyard."

"No," Ramon stated flatly. "He doesn't. It failed. The vineyard in Spain fell apart like every one of his other enterprises." He looked around to the crate with Zoltan's countenance smiling at them. "Two years ago he went bust." Ramon gestured to the box. "He sent you that so you'd think everything was fine with him. You know his pride . . . And he *did* try to make a go of the wine thing. The weather turned on him. The wine crop failed."

Angelina barely made it back to the bed before her legs collapsed from under her. Weakly, she asked, "Where is he now?"

"In Italy. In Borello."

Angelina looked up, alarmed. "Borello!" The village represented an elephant burial ground to their people. It was a medieval town perched high on a rock cliff. To visit it was to fall backward in time. A hundred years behind the rest of the world, the bells of the single church rang every quarter hour, a town crier moved through the streets, and water was fetched at the well in the town square, which was really a circle.

When a Gypsy retired to Borello, even the police did not follow, knowing destiny had left its calling card. Fate had all but put its seal on the grave of the exile. The crippled of spirit went there to live out their days, and the old people went there to die. Zoltan was not old enough to die. He had fallen into the other category. Bent and broken as his soul had to be, through the years of effort and corresponding disappointment of seeing his dreams shattered, Zoltan would never be able to stand straight again. Not after the vineyard . . . that was his last hope.

Tears traced a warm path down Angelina's face. Ramon walked over, brushed them away with an index finger. She knocked his hand aside. Taking no notice of her hostility, Ramon intoned with the softness of a cat's purr, "We can help him." He paused. "I can help him, Angelina, but only if you help me."

He waited, and slowly Angelina raised her eyes. "How?"

And Ramon told her.

He had, in fact, been in America for the very purpose of rescuing their father from his desperate situation. He admitted that at first he was not certain how to go about this. Chivalry was hardly a familiar trait. It had to be grown into. Certainly, as Angelina might suspect, he had invested his time and efforts in a scheme or two, wanting to do things on his own—more or less.

But, alas, they had not turned out quite as he had envisioned; thus, Ramon explained, he was, on occasion, forced to borrow a little something here and there, in order to tide him over until the current went more in his direction.

Angelina grimaced. "And I was just one of the few people you borrowed from. I really could kill you, Ramon! You're so thoroughly despicable."

"Oh, don't!" he pleaded, his usual wicked humor lighting his face. "For then I couldn't pay you back. Nor could I rescue our father."

"Fine," Angelina said, glowering. "Go on, then. Tell me, Ramon. Tell me just exactly how you plan on helping Father."

"Well! I'm glad you're finally showing some interest." Pacing thoughtfully before her, he outlined his scheme. "I've followed your career very closely. What a rise! You have talent and luck on your side! Not to mention beauty. And cunning," he added.

"Forget the cunning, Ramon."

"But, you see, I can't. Clever little Gypsy, to marry one of the richest men in America—perhaps in the entire world."

"He's not rich himself."

"He has access, love. Not just to his family's money, but also to the funds—and possessions—of friends and associates who are in the same league."

"So? Do you think he's going to pass the hat for you, Ramon?"

"For me? No, indeed, not for me." Ramon feigned the wounded look of the unjustly accused. "For Father."

"Look, I had a hard day. I'm exhausted. So just cut all the garbage and get to the point. Remember, it's me you're talking to, not some—"

"Socialite!" he finished for her and pointed a finger at her. "What you will do, now that you are yourself a socialite—not to mention having entrance into the estates and other sundry fashionable residences of those of similar standing—is to provide me with a list of your friends' possessions. Also, it would be helpful to have a physical plan of such real estate in which I might gain safe entrance and safe egress."

"Really?" Angelina said. "Let me see if I've followed you correctly. In essence, you will strip my friends clean of their things. And in doing so, this larceny will help Father immensely. Congratulations, Ramon. You've come up with your most demented plan. You've totally exceeded yourself. Now get the hell out of my life."

"Angelina, Angelina . . . you should have more vision. What I intend is that the goods will be redistributed via, shall we say, a circuitous merchandising route? To good homes in Europe. For a fee, of course. The proceeds of which will go to fund a new enterprise for Father."

"Ah, I see now. Like Robin Hood. That's who you fancy yourself."

"Somewhat, yes. I'd say, certainly there's a similarity. Everyone wins. The rich who have been relieved of a few tired possessions merely report the loss to their insurance agencies, who reimburse them. This allows your friends to go out shopping again—something they all love to do. I've merely given them a way to fill their days."

"You're so good, Ramon."

"Yes, well, I try to help, lightening the loads of others whenever the need presents itself." He nodded, accepting the compliment with a wicked smile. "And then, of course, there are the homes the items will grace, making new owners happy. They'll go out and buy new carpets, paint inside. Oh, there's really no end to what my little scheme will do to help the world's economy.

Besides, we're only talking about things. Just as things are pinched, they're always replaceable.''

"Some things carry meaning in them. They aren't just items to own. Some things may stand for something."

"Oh, Angelina, Angelina . . . you've grown soft."

"David has a clock. It's been in his family for generations. It belonged to Jefferson—a president of this country. It stands for all that's noble and fine. It *means* something, can you understand? A clock like that can never be replaced. It doesn't even have a monetary value."

Ramon's eyes glistened. "You see, what did I say? I was right. You're so astute, little sister. You have picked a man of refinement and ethics. I myself have such aspirations. And this is the beginning."

"No, Ramon. This is not the beginning. Because I'm not going to help you. Now, for the final time, I am telling you—not asking—but telling you to get out of my apartment and stay out of my life."

He didn't budge. "You really have no choice but to help me." Slipping his hand into his back pocket, he pulled out a thin envelope. He handed it to her.

Angelina examined its contents, a collection of newspaper articles related to her upcoming marriage to David. Underlined were all the sections having to do with her family background, all of which were pure invention, a cotton-candy, dream-spun fantasy.

Ramon laughed. "Such a lineage you come from. I had no idea. A family of aristocrats."

"I didn't say that."

"You implied it!" Ramon shot back.

"So? What was I supposed to do! Tell them the truth?"

"The truth! Yes, the truth! That your family does not raise horses; we steal them. That is our past, and in some cases, when necessary...it is our present. Of course, today we prefer a Ferrari to an old nag. But we fit our needs to the occasion as it presents itself. And in this case, you're going to be our family's express transportation to respectability."

"I don't have to ask you what you'll do if I don't go along with your plan, do I?"

"No. I give you more credit than that. You've always been stubborn, never stupid. That's why I know I can count on you. As I said, you have no choice." Ramon kissed her lightly on the cheek. "I'll be back in three days. We'll begin work then. Otherwise, let the headlines fall where they may." He backed away. "What a warmth family closeness brings, eh, Angelina? *Adieu*, Princess."

Ramon swept from the room, for once using the door, which Angelina hastened to lock, as if she might keep him out for good. But behind her the curtains still fluttered, and the papers rustling on the floor seemed to chatter a hysterical message that she would never be able to escape him. He would come through a window. He would come, like some bug, through a crack in the wall. He would pick a lock in a door. He would shimmy down a chimney. But Ramon would come, regardless, to ruin her life.

Chapter Ten

Angelina's jumps were beautifully formed, her beats clean. Each landing was that of a feather. The others in the troupe, standing at the sidelines in relaxed poses, watched in mute astonishment, cognizant of her immense talent that seemed to expand with every day. Sasha, himself, applauded her virtuosity.

Angelina acknowledged his praise with a smile more automatic than heartfelt. After completing her solo she slid her towel off the ballet barre and looped it around her neck to collect the moisture dotting her skin, then retired to the sidelines with the others.

"Hey, that was all right," one of the girls said with a thumbs-up sign.

"Thanks," Angelina returned. "Maybe my turns could have been more precise."

"In another lifetime, hon. They looked as good as any turn's going to get on this planet."

None of them knew. Nobody. Who would suspect by her smiling face, by her perfect leaps, that she had only three days left to be fully alive? Angelina patted her face dry with the light blue terrycloth. She was ready to call it a day and it wasn't even noon yet.

"Angelina!" Sasha called to her as he passed on his way to the pianist in the corner. Their accompanist was busily flipping pages of the new score composed for Sasha's intricate ballet. Sasha's face was alight with mischief as he came close. He whispered so only she might hear, "Later we talk about you to become star of company."

When she did not respond Sasha's face fell. "Your mind flies, Angelina? You do not hear great words I say?"

Clouds parted in her mind just long enough to respond with a dull politeness. "Sorry. What was that?"

"Come! Come now with me!" Sasha said, simmering. He motioned for her to follow. As he strode across the hardwood floor he yelled to the others to break for ten minutes. Bodies dispersed from the room silently. In the hall they could smoke and gossip or dash across the street for gum or candy. Only a fool would hang around when Sasha was in a bad mood. Conversely, when Sasha was enthusiastic about something, he expected others to share in his vision. Woe unto those who crossed him then. Sympathetic eyes flicked Angelina's way. Boy, was she going to get it.

Hardly feeling the floor beneath her, Angelina moved after Sasha to the small office he had put together for himself at the far side of the rehearsal hall.

"So," he said, closing the door. "I give you biggest news of whole life. You say nothing. Because you hear nothing. Your brain is in sky."

"My head," Angelina corrected, "my head's in the clouds. My brain's in my head, and my head is the thing that's..." She stopped. She was becoming a lunatic. Sasha was always mixing things up and always would. It was part of his charm. One just adjusted and shut up about it.

"Well, again I say the news." Sasha pouted. His arms were folded defiantly across his chest. "You are ready to hear now?" Angelina nodded. "Good. The news: you are my new star."

She stared at him, wanting to respond, aware that it was the right thing to be happy; but there was no energy available to feel anything.

Sasha nodded. "Ah, I expect this. Great excitement! You go crazy! The screams! Kisses for Sasha!" He stopped and, looking at her, said, "Okay, I know. You do not believe."

How could she express anything about a future, a fictitious future, when she was not going to be a person after three days? She was going to be a paper cutout. She would have no insides to her, no dimension. She had to say something, though; he was waiting for her to say something.

"That's wonderful. I'm very happy. I'm surprised, and I'm happy. It's...wonderful," she intoned listlessly. "Thank you. Of course."

"Then you will be even more excited with this. The next news: we are going to Paris! We will dance there this year, a permanent company. Great culture. Most important people. All of Europe will be at our heels."

"Feet, not our heels—they'll be at our feet," Angelina corrected, the information he had just imparted only partially filtering through to her. Paris? The company was going to Paris? And she...hadn't she just been told she was to be the star of the company? So that meant that she was to go to Paris, as well.

"So?" Sasha said. "No words come out. You are too excited, no?"

"Thrilled, yes," Angelina said. She was going to Paris to be a paper cutout dancer.

"We will begin there in three weeks. But you must go first. It is for you to rest. The lagging from jet is most difficult. If you are not good in the body, you hurt yourself. Then, future goodbye. So, you rest. And you find good place to live. Organize self to be great star. Oh, and clothes. You must find things to wear to be most beautiful woman in Paris. The peoples, when they see you, they see my great company. You are not just you. You are me. You, Angelina, are not you anymore."

"I know," she said. "I'm not me, anymore." And tears slid down her face.

"Yes," Sasha said gravely, "I know why the tears. I know." He was silent. "This is the bad thing. You get married here, then you leave, you have no marriage. Right, I am? I know, I know...always there is this problem with the dance."

Angelina sniffed, the tears flowing more profusely with every word he uttered reminding her that she would not be getting married.

"But you must choose. Now. You can be woman. Or, you can be legend. You must say now."

Behind Sasha was a famous ballet poster. It showed a dancer hurtling into space, the stars a backdrop for the dancer's amazing grace and strength and beauty. In a way, the representation was a magnificent and thrilling testimony to the ability of man to merge with art and become, almost, more than human. During the long years of ballet practice, a mere glance at this poster would fuel Angelina with enthusiasm to become like the vaulting goddess in the picture. But now there was another quality to the print never before noticed. There was a stark loneliness to the scene. The woman existed in space, infinite space, cold and uncompanionable. And suddenly Angelina realized that all along she had been fooling herself. There would have always been this ultimate choice to make. You could reach the stars, but only alone.

"Yes. Make me a legend," Angelina said. The words rang out in what seemed like a vast hollow space.

There had been no decision to make. Ramon had made it for her earlier.

"The show's going to be incredible," David said that evening in his apartment.

They had both made a special point to be together that night. With their hectic schedules, their time with each other was so precious lately. A simple dinner at a decent hour, when they could both stay awake and make intelligent conversation, took on an almost religious significance. Angelina sat curled at the end of his couch while David placed a cup of coffee on the table before her. He carried his own to the wing chair facing Angelina.

"The enthusiasm from the international art councils is overwhelming," he said. "This exhibition isn't important just for the quality of the work to be shown, but for the amount of cooperation we're all experiencing. I'll tell you something, they can have their great summit talks in Geneva, but where things really come together is when people speak heart-to-heart and share their feelings through the arts. You want some of that coffee cake I picked up?''

He was up, going toward the kitchen before Angelina could even reply that she did not. A dose of hemlock would have been more in keeping with the state of her mind.

Back again, he placed a plate before her, brought his own to the table by the chair, and continued where he had left off.

''Music...poetry...sculpture...paintings. There's the raw proof, the tangible evidence that all people want love and peace. We all want the same things. But we complicate life so. Not in art, though. There it's so simple, so unbelievably plain. I really feel like this is my chance to contribute something to the world. It feels good, this...this...''

''Commitment.'' The word was bitter on her tongue, a cruel joke thrown in her face. God help her, but only a consummate actress—or a Gypsy—would have been capable of maintaining the act she was forced to perform this night. She wanted to rush into his arms and bury herself in his soul so deeply that she could never be taken from him by time or any conditions known to man.

Forever after she would remember David like this: ablaze with energy and love, innocent of the underbelly of life she miserably knew so well. And so unaware of the cold hell to come. Inwardly, soundlessly, she sobbed for the both of them.

As David spoke, points of light flashed to the surface of his eyes, excitement and goodwill bursting out from their depthless green, piercing her, exploding against her aching heart.

How could she tell him she was not going to marry him? *She could not.*

"Angelina," David continued, a change coming to his tone. "I know this season's busy for you. But you must find some time to get to Paris for the show. Oh, I know . . . Sasha. He'll go crazy. But we'll talk to him together. It's not like the Winthrops haven't contributed enough to his company to deserve a favor in return. You've got an understudy. He may not like it, but he'll just have to use her."

"I'll talk to him," Angelina lied.

How David would hate her, and all the more now, for having let things go so far, and then only to walk out in the end! A cruel trick, if ever there was one. That's the only way it would seem.

David would never understand what happened! He *could* never understand. He would never know the truth.

There was simply no way for them to ever be together once he learned the facts of her background. His family would never permit it. If David did, by some miracle, sacrifice his career and his family relationship for their love, he would only end up hating her later. Everything he might have had in life, everything beautiful, his whole carefully conceived "destiny" would have been thrown down the tubes for her. Even if he could live with that knowledge, she couldn't. She loved him too much to destroy him.

"You know, we've never really talked about it before," David was saying. "We've overlooked the matter, but it's got to be faced. I'm going to be gone for quite some time with the exhibit. We'll be apart. I can't even stand the thought of it, Angelina. You're my whole life. To be without you . . . ah, I can't even think of it.

What hell! It'll be like being dead.'' His eyes were filled
with love, his voice, generally so calm, choked with
emotion.

Angelina had to turn away. *Like being dead. Indeed,
my dearest love. Indeed.*

"So," he said quietly, "you know what I'm thinking, what I'm going to ask. I know I've no right. I
mean, I know how much your career means to you.
And I'm so damn proud of you. You're so beautiful, so
talented. Without a flaw! That's what my parents say.
They're so happy that I've found someone who fits in—
their term—that you 'fit in'. From their perspective,
you're an acquisition. You make the family look
good...a woman of the arts, that sort of image. So,
anyway, you'd have to know by now, I'd never ask you
to give up dance, but I'm selfish, I admit it. If I'm to
follow my star, and you're to follow yours, darling,
there's going to be a lot of time and space between us.
So we'll both have to compromise.

"And I will," he said, as if having just reached that
decision. "Dammit, I'll never be one of those louts who
thinks his work is more important than the career of the
woman he loves!''

Angelina hid behind the brim of the coffee cup, her
eyes lowered to hide her anguish.

*Oh, how proud would you be of me, David, if I
marry you, and to keep my brother's mouth closed I
steal from your parents, from all your friends? Oh,
clever, clever Ramon. May he rot—if not in hell, then
somewhere very hot and very miserable.*

"It doesn't matter, anyway," David said. "There's no
obstacle we can't overcome. Love conquers all! We're
going to be the two happiest people alive, Angelina. My

love...we are going to have a lifetime together. And what a lifetime it will be!''

No, my darling, we have only two more days. That is all, just two more days.

Those two days came and went with such cruel rapidity it seemed as if life had conspired to suddenly condense itself. Each second seemed to strain through her heart like grains of sand passing through an hourglass. Each particle of time was so valuable, so transient. Oh, to hold this last glimmer of beauty inside of her forever, to fold these few remaining precious moments into her heart where she might take them out to cherish again and again in the empty years ahead! The agony was beyond any she had known in her entire life. David's face, smiling...the sunlight glinting off his hair as he walked toward her outside of Tiffany's, where they met to pick out their wedding bands together...the happy assurance of his voice as he paid the clerk for their selection.

After Tiffany's, Angelina did not return to rehearsal. Instead she slipped back to her apartment. In less than two hours, she had boxed up her possessions and packed her clothes in a suitcase. Once a Gypsy, always a Gypsy, she considered ruefully. For once she was glad. How easy it was, still, to slip away, to escape an impending unpleasantness without ever facing the situation directly. The Gypsy's way...

Sasha had agreed earlier to have her things shipped to Paris once she had found a new place. He had wanted her to leave at once; and of course, she had to leave.

Well, at least Ramon would be outwitted. That was something. There would be no reward for his treachery when he came to collect. There would be no one there.

* * *

David was late that night. Angelina waited for him to arrive for their planned dinner—their last supper. She stood by the window in his apartment, looking out at the street, seeing the trees for the last time, noticing the cracks in the pavement, the oil stains on the cement, thinking how truly magnificent this view had become now that she would never see it again.

Finally, she saw David. A cab let him out across the street. He paid and, briefcase in tow, moved rapidly across the street. Glancing up, he saw her in the window and a smile came instantly to his lips. He waved. Angelina waved back.

"What's wrong?" he asked, coming directly to her when he entered the apartment.

"Wrong? Nothing. Why, what makes you ask that?" Her heart constricted. What had she given away?

He had her in his arms now, and was kissing her nose, moving his mouth to her neck, playfully nibbling her ear, teasing her, and then the kisses became more serious. Angelina moved into him, pressing herself against his body, her hands desperate for this last feel of his skin, of the smell of his cologne and clothes and . . .

"Angelina?" David asked quietly, and pushed her away slightly with a look of concern. "What is it, darling?"

Angelina shook her head. "Nothing . . . why do you think something's wrong?" Again she moved against him, but he withstood her advance.

"It's something . . . I don't know. Your face—when I waved to you out there, there was this look to you, such sadness. And I can feel it, something . . . you're not just kissing me, you're—"

"Devouring you?" Angelina said, laughing. She spun away so he could not see her distress. "That's because I'm famished and the dinner I made's all but cold. I turned the heat off because it was becoming shriveled."

It worked. David made his excuses again for being late, and she further got him off the track of her strange mood by asking about the meeting that had been responsible for his late arrival.

David was tired that night, actually exhausted. She could see the fatigue in his eyes and in the way he moved. He told her that as each day passed he was becoming more aware of the monumental responsibility he had undertaken in being at the helm of the exhibition. Although drained, he was also wound too tightly to relax properly. He suggested a nightcap of brandy for the two of them before bed.

Angelina finished her glass quickly then slipped beneath the covers, curling against his body as he downed the last of the liquid in his snifter. Luxuriating in the warmth of his skin, she ran her fingers along the length of his hip and upper thigh. David sighed and turned into her, lying on his side as he took her face in his hands and began to kiss her mouth, then the hollow of her neck, then the mounds of her breasts. With the first touch of her hand on his flesh, she felt him harden.

This would be the last time, she thought.

Every movement of his body was like the lick of flame against her soul. "Oh, David . . . my darling . . . I love you so!" she cried out between their kisses.

She yielded to him with a desperation that was in itself a crazy passion. Inflamed by her responsiveness, he matched her raw animal desire with a driving frenzy of his own. Her legs were bands of liquid fire, trembling against his body. Expertly, with hands and mouth, with the urgent insistence of his spiraling body, David played changing melodies on her body. His control over her pleasure was knowledgeable and total. And her willingness to give and take was encouragement to further exploration and triumph.

Trembling together, they drove faster and with a hypnotic precision that made time and space and place dissolve. Only they existed for each other. Only they, exploding in the fire of each other's embrace, could know the glory of that climb into an infinite ocean of pleasure.

"My God, Angelina," David said when they lay sated in each other's arms. "I've never experienced anything like that, not ever, not ever... my love."

Angelina stroked the arm cradling her. Tears trailed along her cheeks. She could not speak, no thoughts could form in this aftermath of the most ecstatic and exquisite moment she had ever known on earth. And there, on the other side of ecstasy, was the cold yawning abyss of the future.

For one insane moment she thought she might tell him everything. "David..." she whispered. But the only response was his breathing, relaxed and even. And then the desperate moment passed and she was again rational.

His deep fatigue made it easy to slip from his side. By his pillow, where her head had lain beside him, she placed the note written earlier. It said only what needed to be said, that she must follow her dream of being a legend, rather than marry him. This was cruel, but it was also plausible, a motive he would accept.

Angelina stood by his bed for a moment, memorizing his face forever in her mind. With her hand on the bedside lamp, she whispered, "My darling...I love you. Forever." With the slightest pressure, the light was extinguished.

Five minutes later Angelina slipped from the front door of the apartment building with her single suitcase in hand. The air that night was warmer than usual. Somewhere nearby a television could be heard and, intermingling with the canned laughter, the sound of soft rock from a radio.

A taxi came into view, cruising slowly with its light on, signifying its availability. Angelina stepped into the street and put her hand out. The taxi stopped and she got in.

"Where you off to?" the driver asked.

"The airport," she said. "Kennedy."

"Vacation?"

"I'm running away," Angelina replied. "I'm a Gypsy. Gypsies always run away in the middle of the night." The man laughed. He didn't believe her.

And Angelina stared out the window, wanting to scream, wanting to die, wanting never to have been born.

Chapter Eleven

David awoke by the clock's alarm at the side of his bed. In the initial haze of coming out of sleep he assumed that Angelina had gone off to the bathroom or the kitchen. He smiled then, exchanging the world of nocturnal fantasies for the warm memories of the lovemaking they had shared the previous night. He drifted pleasantly like that for a moment, but the sounds beyond the bedroom window eventually intruded, pricked his conscience, and the need to get going and contribute some of his own energies to the world's madness took precedence.

Nude, he swung out of the bed and was on his way to the bathroom to shower when he called out, "Hey! I'm sorry! Forgot to tell you. Breakfast meeting at Rockefeller Center this morning. No time for a feast!" He expected a sarcastic reply from the other room, and when only silence followed his announcement, he called, "Angelina?"

This time he poked his head around the corner and called more loudly. "Hey, Angelina? I love you. And I'm sorry about not telling you if you've done something special in there. You can throw it on my head, okay?"

The silence ate his words, and gave nothing back. He walked into the kitchen, but found it empty. It was when he went back into the bedroom that he noted the piece of paper folded over on Angelina's pillow. He hadn't known she was leaving early.

Grabbing his watch from the dresser as he went over to see what message she had left for him, his thoughts strayed to the meeting with the foreign ambassador he would have in less than an hour. But in thirty seconds, his world had changed completely, and no ambassador and no art exhibition and no amount of fame or money could make the world seem remotely right again.

David stood while he could, holding the note between fingers now grown cold. Then his legs seemed to dissolve into bands of rubber and he fell onto the bed, where he sat dumbly, trying to make thoughts come together that would make sense of what he had just read.

It couldn't be true! Just yesterday, not twenty-four hours before, they had picked out their wedding bands! Last night they had made love…God, and what a time it had been! No, he reasoned, thoughts bursting through his mind in wild, staccato impulses, she would be in her apartment now. Perhaps he had said something? Done something? She had taken offense. Women, he understood, were like that—peculiar, mercurial, overemotional creatures. Even Angelina, who had never before displayed such traits, must have suffered some tinge of emotional instability. The rings—perhaps she had been frightened by the realness of it all. He looked forward to the wedding, but then that didn't mean that she might not have jitters. Many people did. His mind raced on, frantic to put order in his life.

He dressed in haste, donning yesterday's shirt, crumpled on the floor from where he had dropped it, slipped into his trousers and, not bothering with socks or shoes, left his apartment to pound on Angelina's door. When there was no answer he tore back to his apartment and got the key she had given him.

A moment later her door was unlocked and he stood within the deserted confines of Angelina's apartment. The only clue that she had once lived there was the mirrored wall with its wooden ballet barre and the boxes packed and sealed, cartons that must have contained her possessions.

The note ending their relationship was still in his hand, clenched in a tortured fist. With a wail of fury and despair and love, he drove the fist against the wall. "Angelina!"

Sasha was in the middle of rehearsal when David appeared. At first he did not recognize him, for the man he knew as Angelina's fiancé was always neatly dressed and certainly clean-shaven. This man, slumping toward him, was everything to the contrary. His clothes might have been fished from a laundry pile and a growth of stubble shadowed his face. In fact, Sasha thought, there was an aura of darkness about David Winthrop's whole personality as he strode obliviously through the center of the dancers who were still attempting to practice, even as they tried to avoid crashing pell-mell into David.

"Where is she?" David demanded when he had reached Sasha.

"Angelina, you mean."

"Where is she? Just tell me. That's all I want to know. I'm going to clear this whole thing up. No one's going to be hurt—I can understand your position. But as good a dancer as she is, she's still only an employee to you. She's my whole life."

Sasha, although Russian, hated angry scenes, especially ones in which he might come to some physical harm. "It was her decision, entirely," he said. "I made her offer to dance in Paris. There was no way she could get to the top of mountain if she does not devote entire being to the dance. This is not job, this is religion. Her talent is great and it is holy."

"I don't care why she left," David said, stepping in closer, as if to do some physical damage. "I want to know where she is."

"Now? She is over Atlantic Ocean," Sasha said, moving back two steps. "I do not have address for her. In Paris she will find a new home. And," he said, "a new life. It is what she wants."

"Bull, it is! I know Angelina. I know the woman I love. And she loves me. I don't give a damn what she told you. And I don't believe the note she wrote me, either."

"Then why?" Sasha sputtered, searching for a way to defend himself. "Why does she leave? To me, she says, 'Yes, I want to be a star—to go to Paris.' To dance on top of highest mountain is what Angelina wants."

"I don't know," David said coldly. "But I'm not going to rest until I find out. And there is a reason. Another one. Not this stupid story about dancing on top of some mountain!" David turned into the quiet of the rehearsal hall. The eyes of every dancer were fixed upon him as he made his way through their midst.

Ramon was dressed in a new pair of eggshell-colored slacks and a polo shirt of the same background color, with a tiny, refined and delicate navy stripe running horizontally through the fabric. Everything he had on that morning was clean and new, from his soft, white, leather yachting shoes to the gold watch to which he had helped himself on the way to cementing his deal with Angelina. This was the beginning of a whole new life for him. In fact, as he walked up the stairs leading to Angelina's apartment building, he envisioned a life-style in the not too distant future in which he would never wear the same outfit twice. He thought, in fact, that he might make white "his" color; a kind of trademark by which he might be remembered. Certainly he would be spoken of and noticed by a great many people. Success brought with it a certain obligation to dress and act the part. He would be an inspiration to others.

A minute later, filled with himself and these accompanying noble intentions to be a role model, he rapped cheerily against Angelina's door. He waited, then tapped again, a little more insistently this time, when she did not spring to answer at once.

"Angelina!" he yelled, not liking the silence. It took him less than forty seconds to jimmy the lock and enter. What he saw made the blood drain from the upper part of his body, and fill his legs with a leaden disappointment that for the moment rendered him immobile. He could only gape at the empty room.

Not being one to fool himself, he identified the situation for what it was. *The clever little bitch had fled!* To think that his own sister could run out on him! It was so unfair. His heart felt like breaking. All of his beautiful plans! Without Angelina he had nothing!

And, it was such a good plan, too. It was maybe the first and only truly excellently conceived plan he had ever had.

In a fury he left her apartment, not bothering to close the door after him. For all her snooty ways, she really had accumulated nothing but rubbish anyway; she was no better than any of their clan when you boiled things right down to their essence. He was licking his psychological wounds as he passed down the hall, thinking of Angelina's haughtiness during their last conversation, when something she had said suddenly entered his mind at the precise second he was in front of David Winthrop's door. It was as if the proverbial Light of Inspiration had flashed in his noggin.

It took him slightly longer to break into David Winthrop's apartment than it had Angelina's, but he managed. There was some danger involved in this trespass, but not much. He knew exactly what he had come for and found it almost at once.

The clock was locked up in a little glass house, which was an annoyance, actually, as it made the theft of the clock less easy to conceal. Besides, Ramon was not keen on jails of any kind, even those that only bound a mechanical object. The very idea of imprisonment drove him wild.

It was a tricky affair, opening the housing, but he was a tricky man. Within minutes, after a few false tries, he had liberated the gold clock. Feeling wonderful, feeling vindicated somewhat, he walked boldly from the apartment carrying his booty in a paper bag he had found in David's kitchen cupboard.

He would not sell this clock. It was too special. Having belonged to a president of the United States! He chose to consider its possession as an omen that things would, indeed, get better for him. The clock was his talisman. Yes, Ramon thought, walking jauntily down the block, Angelina was quite right. There were things that really did not have a monetary value.

And now he, Ramon Zarsuela, had one of them! He was moving up in the world. And sooner or later, he'd fix that Angelina!

David fairly stumbled across the threshold of his apartment when he returned after seeing Sasha. He was that disoriented, that fatigued. He had never realized how draining emotions could be. It was the helplessness that was the worst!

There was simply nothing he could do at the moment but wait. Eventually, Angelina would be found. She would resume rehearsals in Paris with Sasha. It would only be a matter of time before he could clear up the matter. Everything would work out. They would get married and live happily ever after.

Absently, and in search of some normalcy to balance the craziness of his life, he began to clear up a coffee cup left on the table. The cup rattled against the dish, the clatter of a voice, a taunt, which further enervated him. Without Angelina there would be no peace.

Hell! David hurled the cup across the room. It shattered against the fireplace. The pieces flew in a starburst pattern to the floor.

The violence was uncustomary and he was sorry immediately. But nothing about his life seemed customary anymore. Until he and Angelina were reunited, he had no life. His heart pumped madly, grief almost overwhelming him as he moved heavily across the Oriental carpet to collect the damage he had caused.

It was on his way to the fireplace that he saw it. The glass casing of the clock gleamed in its usual place on the table. Only it was empty.

Three days later, the officer from the theft division of the local police precinct visited David's apartment. He took notes as David spoke.

"You noticed it missing three days ago and you just called now? This clock is supposed to be very valuable, right? That's what you just said." The officer poked his pen against the words he had just written on his pad. "You said that."

"I was very upset." David ran his hands through his hair. He had finally showered and shaved and changed into clean clothes that morning. But for the past three days he had eaten only minimally, just enough to keep the hunger pains from turning his stomach; and if he had slept it had been in tortured snatches. Certain his parents would want to know what had happened to him, he'd called and said he was sick and would be sleeping off the flu. His secretary was handed the same story and advised to cancel all of his appointments until further notice. After that he did not answer the telephone.

"About the clock?" the policeman reminded.

"Yes. About the clock. I just couldn't believe it was gone. It's very special to my whole family."

"Insurance?"

"I don't know. I expect there is. But it's not really the money. I can't tell my family, you see. What I want is help in finding the clock. I don't even care about prosecuting the thief. It's the clock I want."

"You've got any ideas? Leads?"

"No."

The officer examined the casing again. "Pretty tricky apparatus here," he said, referring to the locking mechanism on the bottom of the stand.

"Yes, supposedly it was devised by a master locksmith, a man considered in his day to be a genius. It's, I guess, a piece of art in and of itself," David commented.

"Well, one thing's for sure. The clock was taken out by a master thief. No amateur could have figured it out."

"I don't know about that," David said. "My girlfriend figured it out in a couple of tries."

The policeman didn't look up, but something in his voice made David's blood turn cold. "Yeah? So, uh, where's your girl? Maybe we should have a little chat with her."

"She's—she's on vacation."

"Oh. Well, I'll talk to her when she comes back."

When the officer had finally gone, promising to be in touch as soon as they had any leads, David stood alone in his apartment and considered what he had not considered before. Angelina was the only person he had ever known who could open that case without the special instructions.

And now Angelina and the clock were missing.

To his parents, David told this story: "She's in Paris! Sasha sent her over early. The troupe's going to be performing there over the next year, with Angelina as the prima ballerina. Of course I'm thrilled for her. She'll be back for the wedding, and then I'll be going over for the exhibition. It's really a perfect situation."

He thought he sounded convincing enough, and nobody seemed to question him further, except for now and then, to ask what news he had received recently from Angelina. They, of course, fictitiously spoke every night. Money was no object when it came to true love.

Money was also no object when it came to fitting together the missing pieces of the life of the woman he had once loved, and still loved with a torturous intensity that was driving him to distraction.

He had gotten the idea when looking at the shattered pieces of the cup on the floor. It was just a vague impression, an image, really, of a jigsaw puzzle. He felt, as he bent to gather the broken pieces of the cup, that if he could fit the china back together, it would be in some way symbolic of putting together their romance. It was stupid, but nevertheless, the idea of it came to possess him. So, that rather than throwing the pieces away, he laid everything out on a table and would periodically try to make things fit.

On one occasion, while brooding over his inability to discover an odd, missing shape, he thought that he had been similarly unsuccessful in discovering details from Angelina's past. It was, he began to muse, possible that there was something in her past that would be a link to her present behavior.

On his own, he tried to trace down members of a Zarsuela family belonging to Angelina. All his efforts yielded empty results. It was maddening. It seemed as if anything and everything she had told him had been a lie.

Was their love a lie, too? He was desperate to find something of Angelina that bore substance.

He had been reluctant at first to implement the investigation, feeling it was a betrayal of Angelina's desire to keep her past buried. But his need to understand their relationship went beyond this loyalty to her wishes, and one day he took the step that he decided was necessary.

The agency was rated as the finest investigative service in America. The director had once been a head of a top governmental investigative bureau, and he had since worked on what David knew to be highly sensitive cases.

Two weeks after his initial visit, in which David had explained all he knew of Angelina, he received a call from the agent handling the case.

David sat across the rosewood desk, waiting while the investigator opened a file. He looked up to David, saying, "I think the mystery has ended, Mr. Winthrop."

There was something in the man's tone that made David wonder if he really wanted to have his answer.

"Here," the man said, and held the report out to David. "I think by reading this, you'll find the information conclusive."

David took it. "What's the bottom line?" David asked. "She's married? What is it?" His mouth had gone cottony. The man seemed to sense it and handed David a glass filled with water from a tray on the credenza behind him.

The man smiled and settled easily into his chair. "Nothing so dramatic as all of that," he said. "But in your position, I think it will certainly make a difference in your future relationship." He paused. "Angelina Zarsuela is a Gypsy."

David laughed. "No, really."

"Really," the investigator repeated.

"A what!"

"A thief. A drifter. A fake. In a word, simply...a Gypsy. That, Mr. Winthrop is your bottom line."

Chapter Twelve

Angelina folded the international newspaper and put it into the seat pocket of the Boeing 727 that was about to land in Rome.

She turned her head away from the passenger beside her and stared out the window, seeing nothing through her tears as she tried to maintain control of her emotions. Of course she had expected the news, but seeing it there in black and white made it all the worse. And so soon, too!

The article announced that her marriage to David was called off. It was accompanied by a photograph of the two of them together, taken on the night their engagement was officially announced. Professional reasons were cited for the breach.

She had flown to Paris a week before and found a place to stay. It was a beautiful flat, overlooking the Seine. Ordinarily she would never have afforded such luxury. In this case, she was able to sublet the property at a reasonable rate from an opera star on a year's world tour. Once settled, Angelina made the decision to visit Zoltan in Borello.

In the airport, she passed quickly through Immigration and Customs, then arranged for a rental car to drive the six hour distance from Rome to the mountain village retreat, inland from the Adriatic.

For a long while, as she drove, the terrain continued flat and without drama, the region primarily devoted to farming. Although not yet parched as it would be during the summer months, the emerald carpet of the Italian countryside was already fading. Eventually the monotonous landscape gave way to rolling hills terraced with vineyards and olive groves. Shepherds herded their ambling flocks down the middle of the road, oblivious of traffic stalled and waiting behind for passage.

Nothing had changed here since her girlhood, Angelina thought. A feeling of coming home filled her and for a moment sweet memories merged with the relentless ache of her impossible love for David.

At last, in the Abruzzi region, the ascent began. The red Fiat climbed continuously, snaking through dark tunnels and curving along corridors wrapped around the sheer profiles of mountains. Every so often signs would warn of the danger of falling rocks, and periodically there would be recent evidence strewn across her path that the reminder was worth heeding.

If nothing had altered since her own childhood, it could also be claimed that very little, if anything, had changed in any of the innumerable small towns perched high on the edges of mountains in a few hundred years. Some villages had been destroyed by earthquakes, and had been rebuilt over the past century, but many of the dwellings were born in an entirely different era.

Borello, itself, was almost completely intact, three hundred years of history barely touching its architecture, nor showing itself in improved amenities. As Angelina approached from below, the village gleamed in the sunlight, the ice cream colors of its narrow three-story homes, each dwelling leaning upon the next, standing out against the stark majesty of the Central Apennines.

There was a main thoroughfare, narrow, paved, and pitted, running through the village. It was almost five o'clock by the time the Fiat drove slowly down the town's central path. She smiled as she passed the Great Bar, as it was called. It was the only bar, actually, and primarily served ice cream and soft drinks. Its unofficial purpose was as principal meeting place for the town's gossips, of both sexes, who gathered there on schedule, several times a day and deep into the night. Winter or summer, most of the activity took place outside the bar—which was no more than a small plain room with a counter and freezer—where tables were set up for animated card games.

Now, as Angelina passed, the many curious eyes of the gossips followed her progress with interest, no doubt speculating on her identity—for it had been years since she had been there—and her purpose in coming to their village. Even over the engine's hum Angelina heard the gossips' voices buzzing like a giant bee.

She parked the Fiat close to the wall of the Zarsuela's Italian sanctuary. It was a salmon-colored building that rose up three stories to a peaked red-tiled roof. Black wrought-iron balconies fronted the second and third stories with open shuttered doors.

As Angelina left the car, the bells of Borello chimed the quarter hour, just as they had for centuries. Two goats clattered by, looking over their shoulders at a dog who was in turn followed by its master on a donkey.

Looking up, Angelina saw a shadowy form retreat quickly from the window high overhead. She was being observed by someone within. Although she rapped on the downstairs door, no one came to greet her and she finally pushed the door forward, entering the small foyer on her own. Ahead was a narrow staircase leading to the home proper, which was contained on the second and third levels; to the right was a room, once actually a stable housing horses. In more modern times, its use had been converted to a root cellar. Through its open door, Angelina could make out bouquets of garlic and peppers hung upside down, and the dank smell of moist earth mingling with a pungent odor of fermenting wine.

When she reached the second level, she called Zoltan's name. Hearing no response, she went through the three small rooms, and still finding no one, followed the tile stairs to the third story.

She found her father there. He was quickly moving about his bedroom. She had caught him as he changed into another outfit. A rumpled shirt and grimy pants had been kicked to a corner of the room. Even from the doorway, Angelina made out the heavy liquor smell of his breath.

Her father stared at her, his eyes wide with an expression combining guilt and shame and love and excitement all in one glance.

He dropped the suspenders he had been about to pull over his shoulders and ran to her with open arms.

"This is a surprise!" he exclaimed, gladness in his voice. "There would have been a party. Everyone would have come. Today," he went on, trying to hide his humiliation with nonchalance, "was not a good day. Usually I dress…" He gave another shove with his foot to the discarded outfit, as if to banish a loutish associate who had come to discredit him.

An hour later the two of them sat opposite each other in the small second-level kitchen. The meal of pasta and chicken had been prepared by a neighbor woman, a widow with an eye on Zoltan, who had lost Angelina's mother to pneumonia when Angelina was still a child.

"I know everything," Angelina began. "So we don't need all this play acting. Not with me, please, Father. Ramon told me what happened with the vineyard. And it wasn't your fault. I'm sure that it would have worked out, had it not been for nature's interference. You could have told me, you know. I'm a big girl now."

Zoltan gnawed on a piece of chicken, dropped the bone onto his plate and then, clamping greasy fingers around a small glass tumbler, downed a half glass of local wine in one swig. He patted the liquid away with his sleeve.

"And you? You are doing well?" he asked, drawing the topic away from himself.

Angelina told him about her career and nothing about her personal life. There was nothing Zoltan could do to change anything. If he knew the real story, he would feel badly on two counts: that she was ashamed of her family, and that she had reason for that shame.

"But you?" Angelina prodded again, after they had finished discussing her life.

Zoltan's eyes dropped. He shrugged and reached for the wine. Angelina put her hand over his, staying it, and said, "Father, you have never given up, not ever. And you won't this time, either. I know you can start again. You were a success. It was just cut short, that's all. If you begin again with something, this time it will work. I know it will."

Zoltan looked at her directly. "No," he said. "No. I am no longer a young man. Look at me!" He leaned back in his chair, arms extended, displaying himself as evidence.

In truth, Angelina had to admit to herself there was a change in him. Partly physical, looking older and weary, there was also a more alarming alteration. It was his diminished spirit that most worried her. Always, her father had been a fiery, electric presence from whom others recharged themselves. But no longer. Zoltan appeared defeated; there was nothing left in him to give to others. Even Angelina had to face the facts.

"So?" he inquired. "Tell me, what do you see?"

"My father, a wonderful man. A man I love."

"So," Zoltan said, nodding. "Then you do see. I have come here to die."

"Don't be ridiculous!" But she was frightened to her core.

"There is no more energy left in these old bones. And new young bones, they clatter about me, rattling like sabers. It is that damn Antonio!" exploded suddenly, popping out of his chair and going to the shuttered door, where he looked out past the balcony. "How I would like to see his face in the mud," Zoltan muttered with a slice of the old vengeance. "On his knees to me! He says I am old and soft...maybe he is right...but he does not need to say so. That is his biggest fault, his tongue. This big-mouthed squash head! He says he should lead now. He should lead . . . imagine that, nothing but a squash for a head and he thinks he could be king," Zoltan repeated, glowering. But his shoulders had slumped inward and the brief flare of the old recognizable spirit dimmed and grew dormant again.

During the next three days Angelina heard the Borello gossip for herself. Zoltan was perceived by at least half the Gypsies he had governed as being ineffective. He had spoken so long of a different way, of a "legitimate" way, but with nothing to show for it, that no one wanted to hear his pipe dreams anymore. In the past, although they had doubted the possibility that such a radical departure from their traditional ways would work, they had gone along with him, supporting his various enterprises as they materialized. The wine fiasco, as they called it, was the last straw. Clearly, by proof of this latest disaster, it was shown that the Gypsy was not meant to adopt the ways of ordinary citizens.

And Antonio, preening and strutting, loudly promised they would embark on new adventures under his expert guidance, and money would flow as easily as the wine they drank in Borello.

On the morning of her departure to France, Angelina pleaded with Zoltan for the hundredth time to come with her. She was desperate to get him out of the "burial ground" before he completely succumbed to his melancholia. "You don't need them. You can start a new life, free of everything and everyone. Soon I'll have a bit of money ahead and together we can make investments in stocks and perhaps even start a business of some sort."

But nothing she could say or do made any difference.

Her last sight of him was in the rearview mirror of the Fiat. He stood alone on the small balcony, watching her drive away. Still a big man, his shoulders drooped and his chest bowed slightly inward. His jet hair had grayed and his jaw, which had once jutted out to meet any obstacle with proud defiance, rested slack in his face. He seemed, standing there, a man disoriented. In a body he scarcely recognized as his own, he no longer fit in a world that had outgrown him.

It took less than six weeks for Angelina to capture the hearts of the Parisians.

The papers were filled with rave reviews. She had brought all the qualities inherent in a Gypsy—flash, soulfulness, fire, native instinct to seduce—to her dancing roles. But her real conquest was on a personal level. Word was out that the star of Sasha Petrovsky's ballet troupe was beautiful and young and vibrant; in other words, possessed of every quality the French adored.

"The Goddess" one paper had seen fit to call her. Others followed suit, every reporter scrambling to pay the new celebrity homage.

"How long do you think all of this will last?" Angelina asked Sasha, with an ironic smile. She referred to the latest round of accolades bestowed by her adoring press. She and Sasha were in her dressing room after a performance. The room was jammed from end to end with flowers.

"As long as you last," Sasha assured her. "You will not be long to get ready?" he prodded.

"Oh, must I go tonight?" Angelina sighed. "I'd love to go home and just . . . do nothing."

"Not possible," Sasha said. "The party is for you."

"It is not!" Angelina said. "It's for the Belgian ambassador."

Sasha waved his hands. "But he is coming only because you will be there. You are the nip for the cat."

"The catnip."

"Yes. What I said." Sasha bustled over to the rack that held several of her personal gowns. They were all purchased recently. She had gone on a shopping spree overseen by Sasha himself, who, apparently, did not trust her to be the architect of her own image. "This one," he said, and slipped a red liquid-satin floor-length evening dress away from the others. It had a plunging V-neckline and puffed sleeves dropping from below the shoulders. "And . . . and . . ." He hurried off to another corner of the room, where he opened the top drawer of a small chest and extracted a flat box containing a necklace and earrings. "Perfect," he said, placing the stones against the dress. "Too bad they are fakes. Someday real rubies and diamonds."

"Then you'd better raise my salary."

"No, no." Sasha made a reproachful noise. "Some man will give to you. He will see you, and the heart of his will go shopping."

"Oh? Not until the body of this will go to bed with body of his, I think." Angelina mimicked Sasha's thick Russian accent. "And that," Angelina said, finished with her street makeup and swiveled around on her makeup stool, "will never happen."

"You do not like expensive things?" Sasha asked wondrously.

"I do not go to bed with men I don't love."

"Then you must fall in love. With nice gift, comes love very quick. Old Russian saying. Wise, I think."

"American saying: never listen to old Russian sayings. Create much mess in one's life."

Sasha left her alone to dress. But all along the words of their silly conversation intruded upon more serious concerns. She would never go to bed with anyone she did not love; and she would only love one man forever—a man she could never have. At night she lay awake, torturing herself with memories of her lovemaking with David. She heard his voice, could almost will her imagination into feeling the firm warmth of his body lying over her again. But in the morning she awoke alone, restless of body and cold of spirit. And it would always be so.

The party was typical of others Angelina had grown accustomed to attending. There were the usual several heads of state sipping champagne, clinking glasses with practiced smiles and avoiding any kind of direct statement in conversation, and the wives of robber baron industrialists who compared diamonds and spoke of good deeds and great art and of the next party to come.

Sometimes, behind her own smile, Angelina ironically thought: if they only knew they had a Gypsy in their midst, a woman born to thievery and shame of a different level! How accepting would they be of her then?

But in her red dress, Angelina moved comfortably about them. She might have been born to such a role, so easily did she converse and drift and smile and disengage herself from bores and lechers. In her own way, she, too, was a head of state, or at very least might be considered as a lobbyist for the cause of Sasha's ballet company. To this crowd she represented the living embodiment of culture: she possessed talent and physical beauty and refinement. None of these particular qualities were for sale on the open market. A person either earned them or didn't have them. The best this group could do was to rub elbows with the artistically gifted, and at any party artists of various disciplines were displayed as jewels.

"I've just been told!" gushed one social maven, who in her obvious state of excitement almost crashed into two women speaking to Angelina. They all turned their attention to the newcomer. "David Winthrop has arrived in Paris. Just confirmed by my husband."

"But there was that talk about him not coming. I thought it was decided..."

At the mention of David's name Angelina felt her entire body weaken. It was as if every bit of energy had drained from her. She wanted to flee, to run and scream and cry and rail against the gods who had cast her into such a damned role. But all she could do was stand there, with the proper vacuous expression, a butterfly with broken wings pinned to the blank gray wall of existence. There was simply nowhere to run. There was no scream she could wail that would be fierce enough to release the endless sorrow and the pent up passion existing in her. *Oh, David... David...*

"Wasn't his brother coming? You know, the one who had that terrible thing with that Mafia woman?"

"I heard that, yes. But my husband said it simply didn't work out. At the last minute, it was David Winthrop who absolutely *had* to come. I expect he knew more about everything than anyone else. He's terribly clever, I understand. Besides attractive."

"I'll invite him to the garden party."

"Oh, do!"

"Where's he staying? I hate calling at work, through all those little secretaries."

"A pied-à-terre in the Place des Vosges. Henri will get the information for me, and I for you!" Like news reporters preempting a "scoop" on their competitors, the two socialites exchanged congratulatory smiles of collusive triumph. They would snare the season's most eligible bachelor for what Angelina knew to be the season's most lavish social engagement.

"Oh, my..." one of the women said, stopping suddenly to gape at Angelina. "I'm so dreadfully sorry."

"Oh, yes!" joined in a second.

"How cruel, how... well, I'd completely forgotten, you see. I hope the situation won't be uncomfortable for you, my dear."

Angelina smiled a brilliant and empty smile. "Of course not."

"Well, the relationship *was* over."

"Exactly," Angelina said, "and life does go on, doesn't it? For both David and me."

"Then you'll come, too?"

"Of course I will. Why wouldn't I?" Angelina replied with amazement.

But alone that night, in tears, she struggled out of her dress and threw it against the foot of her bed. Of course she would not go to their stupid garden party! Of course she would die first! She did not know how she would avoid David, but she would find a way. The notion of seeing David across a room, his arm around another woman, made her wild with jealousy and despair! Until that moment she had never really considered the possibility—the probability—of David becoming involved with another woman. For her, even if she could not be with David, there could never, ever conceivably be any other man in her life. As melodramatic as it might seem, he was her one and only great love.

On the other side of Paris, in a magnificent town house located on the northwest corner of the Place des Vosges, David struggled with his own impossible situation.

He had done everything in his power to avoid coming to Paris. Yet here he was. The feelings he was experiencing were no easier, and perhaps even worse, than those he had anticipated when he had plotted to escape his responsibility to his family, and on a broader scale, to the international art community.

At first, after his breakup with Angelina, he had attempted to adopt a professional attitude in regard to carrying out his part in the cultural exchange program. But it was impossible to ignore the media's ongoing accounts of Angelina's success in Paris. They did, after all, travel in the same cultural spheres and Angelina was an entertainment phenomenon.

Because he had realized the futility of any attempt to ignore her totally, due to the blitz of stories, he sought to attack the problem head-on. For a weeks' period he subjected himself to the tortuous proposition of actually sitting down each day and reading accounts of her professional and social life unfolding in Paris. He forced himself to examine pictures of her shot while on stage and those showing her shopping or at a gala charity function. It was clear she had no bad camera angle; Angelina was as breathtaking to behold from any view. It was also exceedingly clear to David that no matter what she had done and no matter what she was, he was still in love with her. From the amount and severity of pain he endured in those daily reviews, he felt he would always love her. That it made no rational sense was beside the point entirely: he loved her.

His experiment to burn misery from his soul by the use of misery, did not work. In the end he gave up any hope of getting his Gypsy lover out of his heart or mind. At night he would lie awake, his soul bleeding with pain and eyes moist from the memories of his life with Angelina. In the morning he moved about, appearing to all like any ordinary man with purpose and a future.

Some weeks earlier, he had had a tense conversation with his parents. He had admitted he was an emotional coward, that it would deeply pain him to be in Paris, in the proximity of the woman he had loved, and that for the first time in his life he was refusing to do what they had ordered. He would not go to Paris. Let his brother go.

Two benefits were initially accomplished from this conversation: for one, David felt that he had at long last seized control of his own life in establishing with his parents that he was, indeed, an individual and not part of a mass personality known as a "Winthrop"; and, second, he had accomplished his goal of resigning from his post as head of the cultural exchange art exhibition.

By the end of the second week of his freedom, it was, however, plain to anyone connected to the project, that his brother was unable to take command. It was a combination of temperament and politics, and also simply the basic fact that there were too many tangled threads to unravel at this point that made the show's future doubtful unless David were to again take the helm.

Too many people had contributed too much of themselves for him to refuse for his own selfish reasons. David had felt he'd had no choice but to step back into his old office.

Now, in Paris, David moved to the window of his third-floor study and, pulling aside the velvet drapes and the sheers beneath, looked out upon the square below. In the glow cast from streetlamps he could make out the fountain and see a couple moving across the green to the other side of the street. Somewhere in this same city, the woman he had loved so completely—and would continue to adore until his last breath was taken—would be smiling her enchanting Gypsy smile at some other poor victim of love.

What, David mused, would she steal from him? As for the missing clock, he would have gladly parted with it and a thousand others even more valuable, had she only stayed, had she only left his heart intact.

Somewhere in the city, Angelina stood, laughing, and she still had his heart tucked in some fold of her Gypsy soul.

Chapter Thirteen

The last person Angelina expected to see at her door was the man standing there. She started to slam the door in his face, but he was, as usual, too quick even for her.

"Get out!" Angelina said forcefully.

Ramon proceeded past her, into her apartment. He spoke over his shoulder, both hands held high in the air as if a weapon was pointed at his back. "I come in peace, sister, dear."

"You come in trouble, brother, dear." Having no choice, she closed the door and followed Ramon into the living room. He was peering about, hands in his expensive slacks, taking in the antiques.

"Nice," he said, smiling at Angelina, who did not smile back.

"None of this is mine."

"Yes, I know," Ramon said in more of a business tone.

"And it's not going to be yours, either. What do you mean you know?"

"I keep track. You know how much I care about you. I would never allow anything concerning your welfare to escape my attention." He dropped into a plush powder-blue velveteen sofa, its cushions deep and soft. He spread his arms over the back, relaxing as if he were a valued guest.

"I'll just bet," Angelina commented, not sitting. "Now, tell me what you want and then get out of here. I have things to do this morning."

Ramon glanced at his watch. "Ten. I'll be out by ten-thirty. I promise. But you must listen to me—at least give me a chance. Agreed?"

Angelina sank down in a chair opposite him, her compliance implied.

"Father is in Paris," Ramon said. This immediately got Angelina's attention, exactly as he had intended. "Now, then, the reason Zoltan has been successfully coaxed out of Borello is because of me. I have instilled in him the will to give life another go." Ramon's voice drifted into a lower octave. In a tone of confidence, he said, "He was dying, Angelina. Maybe not physically, but that would be soon to follow given the course of things. Antonio, that overaged brat, has all but taken over!"

Angelina avoided the topic of Antonio. "Exactly what kind of lure did you use to save Father's life?" she asked, the sarcasm thick.

"You simply won't give me any credit, will you? Well, it so happens I've had a change of vision. I've decided that you and father were both right. I'm too old to continue this running and hiding, these hit and miss enterprises. Like you, sister, I want some stability. I want a future that is solid and dependable.''

"Oh, Ramon, please . . . give me a break!''

"That's just it! I want a break. Look, I've got a place already rented in the Saint-Germain des Prés. An antique shop. And I've got a few items already in it as consignment pieces. Because,'' he emphasized, "I knew you wouldn't believe this was for real unless there was some sort of physical proof. Our father is going to run it. And I'll be in charge of acquisitions.''

At that point, Angelina, who had finally begun to listen attentively, began to laugh. "I'll bet you'll be in charge of acquisitions! Through someone's back door and out a side window!''

"No,'' Ramon said, and here his mood also changed. He hung his head and, clasping his hands together, leaned forward and spoke in a soft voice, as close to sincerity as Angelina had ever heard come from him. "I want to do everything the right way. Everything will be—must be!—legitimate. You may not think much of me, but I love Zoltan. He's so beaten down. And without this to look forward to, I'm sure he's going to give up on life entirely. This is my chance, Angelina. I can maybe make up for all the bad I've done in my miserable life. And, I can do something for my father. And,'' he raised his eyes, the rims of which were red, "I can maybe change your mind about your rotten, good-for-nothing brother. I respect what you've done, Angelina. Every day I read the papers and every day my heart swells with pride that you are my sister—the one who is so beautiful, so talented, so—''

"Well-connected? Isn't that what this is all about, Ramon?''

"Well, yes." He smiled. "You are clever, Angelina.
I always tell you that."

"Yes, you do, and I am. I'm also experienced. With
you."

"All right. What you suggest is true. I could use your
contacts. But not for any nefarious purposes, as you
suppose." Ramon rose and began to stroll the room,
touching various vases and figurines, running a finger
over an inlaid table, fingering the pages of a leather-
bound book lying on a shelf. "All I want is that you
give me leads, clues, if you will, to what sort of things
your elegant new friends own and therefore might like.
I'm just asking for information regarding their taste.
And maybe—but not absolutely necessary!—introductions."

"No introductions."

"Okay." He came forward, hope etched on his
handsome face. "But you will, at least, help me with the
other information."

Angelina waited a long moment before replying. It
was not much he asked from her, really; and, it might
help Zoltan to finally establish himself as the great vi-
sionary he had always wanted to be for his people. A
fine antique dealership in the city of Paris would make
the dream a reality and kill the threat of Antonio
usurping Zoltan's rightful place once and for all. It
might be her father's last chance. Suspicious though she
was, she could not deprive him of that chance.

"All right, Ramon. I'll do what I can for you."

Ramon smiled, sunlight breaking in his eyes. Angelina turned and opened the door for him. "And now,
your part of the bargain. Time to go."

Ramon saluted her, and as he passed from the apartment his walk was more jaunty than cat-sly.

* * *

"I simply can't go, that's all," Angelina insisted into the telephone for the tenth time as Sasha insisted otherwise.

"But I am sick. You must!"

"Sasha, I don't care if you are dying—I'm still not going."

"If you do not, then we will certainly lose one-hundred-thousand-dollar grant from Count Duvier. He has picked garden party to make big statement to all big frogs in lake. And how it will be? No one from ballet there to smile and fall down on knees. One-hundred thousand dollars!"

Even Angelina could see his point. As good as the company's box office had been, ballet certainly didn't have the financial base of a rock concert. They would always be beholden to financial handouts from the wealthy if they were to survive. It was a fact of life anyone in the arts had long since been forced to accept. "You're quite positive, Sasha, that there is no way you could possibly hobble over to the affair this afternoon?"

"I swear," he intoned with solemnity.

Angelina sighed. "You don't know what you're asking."

Silence. "David. It is for him you do not want to go."

"Yes, yes, Sasha. I don't want to see him."

"Someday you must. Will happen, Angelina."

"I know. But I'm not ready yet. I need more time."

"There is no time. Put on dress and go." Sasha dropped the phone into the cradle, severing their connection.

The party was held at an estate an hour's drive from the city. It was a medium-sized but nevertheless magnificent palace in terms of architecture, once reputedly inhabited by Henry IV's mistress, Gabrielle d'Estres. The month was June and flowers already abounded in the gardens. From where Angelina stood on a gravel path just outside the palace's formal back entrance, she could view a large pond in which white swans gracefully floated, unperturbed by the revelry taking place above. There were several tents of varying sizes set up to serve refreshments and a large pavilion in which a wooden floor had been placed for dancing. Angelina, who had not been prepared for the day's event, had rushed to ready herself, but arrived late anyway. Now the party was in full swing. The air vibrated with music from the dance floor and the soft early summer's breeze carried the scent of expensive perfume along with the sound of laughter.

She made her way through the throngs of festively dressed guests, her eyes searching for the count who would be expecting Sasha. By now their benefactor was, no doubt, concerned by the dance director's absence.

Her dress was chosen in haste, but was nevertheless appropriate for the outdoor occasion. It might have graced a garden party of an earlier era, designed as it was to touch inches above her ankles. The fabric was a feather-light tulle. Against a background of ivory, the washed impressions of flowers were woven into a design faintly Oriental. The bodice was square, neither adventurous nor modest. It had a dropped waistline outlined in a wide pink satin sash. The skirt lent the most drama to the outfit, falling as it did in various layers of tulle, to appear almost like handkerchiefs fastened at angles.

In another area of the party, David stood as part of a circle of men and women who attended his every word as they might a prophet's. Bored by the sound of his own voice, he droned on automatically, answering their questions about the upcoming art exchange. Now and then his eyes, like his mind, would drift beyond the immediate sea of bodies to where the white swans glided.

He was in midsentence, answering a question about the Russian's last minute agreement—actually, their insistence—to send a painting, when he lost his train of thought.

Standing by the lake's edge were a man and woman. Judging by the slant of their bodies, they were engaged in intense conversation. The woman's dress lifted provocatively in a sudden gust, and she quickly moved to resettle the folds of material close to her body. In the next second she tossed her head and turned, facing David's direction.

Angelina.

For a moment, David stood stunned by her amazing beauty amid the sunlight and greenery, the blazing frontage of flowers, and the background of swans. Even the white billowing clouds overhead seemed to conspire to add to her exquisite form. Hypnotized by the unexpected moment, he could not draw his glance away from her until the woman beside him actually shook his arm.

"Forgive me," David said, and broke away from the circle. In truth, he did not know where he was going, only that he needed some sort of physical activity to break the seizure of panic. He felt, at once, like running and hiding, and at the same instant he wanted to confront her, the devil that she was! He wanted to strike out with some violence against all she had done to ruin both their lives with her deceit.

He went one way, then the other, crazily unable to make up his mind what to do.

Finally, exhausted by indecision, he turned back and strode the incline in the direction of the lake.

She was coming up the gravel path, alongside a middle-aged man with a narrow face and long thin nose; by type, some remnant from medieval French aristocracy, David appraised. That a man was in Angelina's presence was an annoyance. It was even somehow, irrationally, a personal affront.

She had not yet looked ahead. Her face was turned to the side, with her interest seemingly absorbed by her companion's conversational skills, so that David's presence two feet before her, came as a shock.

"I want to talk to you," he said to her. It was a command, rather than a suggestion.

She might have been a doe, about to run. Before she could, David grabbed her arm, and yanked her from the side of the alarmed man accompanying her.

"Do you think . . . ?" the man started, looking helplessly to Angelina for a clue as to the appropriate course of action.

"She doesn't think anything. I'm taking her into those woods where I'm going to throw her to the earth and have my way with her. Several times. You and I can meet out here later with pistols. My second's up there. He'll handle all the details."

"Are you mad?" the man asked stiffly.

"Yes, quite mad. Totally nuts, as a matter of fact," David replied.

The man promptly scurried off, leaving them alone.

David glared at Angelina. He nodded slowly, running his eyes down her form and back to her face. "So. My little Gypsy."

Angelina did not look away, but remained mute. He had never seen her indefensible before. It didn't matter. He had suffered enough to earn the right to be the bully.

"Those black eyes," he said, feeling them burn against his soul. Dangerous emotions churned within, as he felt himself longing to once again drown in their depths, without care and knowledge of who and what she was. Ignorance, sweet ignorance! "I guess I should remember to be careful around you, shouldn't I? Gypsies—dangerous creatures, adept at spells, at thievery. Experts in all forms of treachery. Or so I've been led to understand."

"Stop it!"

"Why? Is holding up the truth to you, so painful, Angelina? Don't tell me you aren't immune to feelings?"

"What do you want from me? It's over! And I don't need these insults. Just let me go." She tried to flee, but he yanked her arm back.

Her black eyes were wild now. "I'm sorry!" she cried out. "If you only knew. Oh, David I am so unbelievably sorry. But what can I do about all of it now? There was never any hope from the beginning. I deluded myself. I kept thinking that somehow my entire history would dissolve and we'd live happily ever after. Of course it was all impossible, and for all the reasons you must have figured out. Being a Winthrop and all," she finished, not sparing him her own brand of bitter sarcasm.

"Yes. Well, as long as you make a pretty apology out of it. I mean, that solves everything doesn't it?"

"How did you find out?"

"What difference does it make?"

"It was because I didn't want you to know that I left," Angelina said miserably. "I wanted you to just remember me as . . . me."

"Next you'll be saying you really loved me."

"I did. I did love you. God, David . . . how could you doubt that?"

David turned his head away, the explosive anger turning rapidly into the longing for what had been lost between them. "Do you have any idea what that did to me, Angelina? Leaving like that. Just walking the hell out of my life!" He drew his eyes back to her. "Can you even possibly imagine how much I loved you and how much I suffered?" He grabbed her shoulders, wanting to shake her silly, wanting to throw her to the ground and walk away from her forever. Instead he brought her roughly up against him and in a surge of emotion kissed her. Months of suppressed sexual passion and anger and love melded into one emotion as he brought his lips against hers.

Angelina struggled to free herself from him. "No, David . . . don't make things worse."

"Worse?" David laughed without humor, and let her go. The passion was slow to subside, and now he felt even more rotten than before. The embrace had been desperate with hunger and fury. And the love was still there ripping at his gut. Stepping slightly back to protect himself from making an even greater victim of himself, he asked acidly, "How could anything have been worse? You leave me. You steal from me—"

"What?" She felt dizzy, as if having been hit. "Steal from you? What are you saying? Tell me, tell me . . ." she urged wildly.

"The clock? Jefferson's clock. Remember it, Angelina? Remember how easily you figured out the locking mechanism? Well, the clock suddenly disappeared when you did. A tidy coincidence. And nervy. I would have thought you'd be smarter. But you knew I wouldn't go after you to prosecute.''

She wasn't seeing David anymore. His words were still coming through, but on another level she was frantically chasing down the corridors of her mind. Ahead, always just out of reach, was the shadowy answer she sought. And then, suddenly, it was there in her grasp.

Quietly, with dignity, she said, ''I didn't take your clock. You can believe that or not. But it happens to be the truth.''

''Can you give me one good reason why I should think so?''

''Yes. You know what you felt with me. And you had to know what I felt for you. The only person you can really ever trust is yourself. So? Do you trust your own feelings?'' Angelina backed away, her eyes glistening with unshed tears. Then she turned and started to run up the hill.

David remained where he was, watching as the filmy layers of her skirt floated around her long slender legs and sunlight glinted against her thick blue-black hair. For a second, his eyes roamed ahead to where gay banners flew from the peaks of the striped tents and guests milled about in constant motion. It might have been a scene from another time. And, looking at Angelina again, he saw her through different eyes, without an emotional filter. There in the countryside she was a wild, free creature, pagan and natural, belonging with the music and the breeze; a Gypsy woman. It was easy to see now.

As he watched her drift into the crowd and disappear from view, his heart took another dive. Why the hell couldn't he let her go? Protect yourself, man! Forcing himself, he dredged up the words the investigator had spoken that day in his office.

"My advice to you, Mr. Winthrop—forget the woman. I know these people. Mostly they're petty criminals. They have no honor. Sometimes, it's true, they can seem an attractive lot. A lot of energy, a certain excitement in being around them. But they're a breed apart from the rest of the human race. They'll use anyone they can. Cheat and rob and blow out of town on the next wind. This one's already shown her colors. Forget Angelina Zarsuela."

God only knew he had tried, David thought as he started up the hill. Only he had failed.

Chapter Fourteen

It was two days before Angelina could implement her plan. First, she needed the address, and then she needed the fortitude to go back on her moral principles. But when she had finally made her decision, she was determined to carry out her mission with skill.

It took her a while to find Ramon's apartment. As she had suspected, it was located in a questionable neighborhood, and in an area with many winding streets, one off-shooting the next. Ramon always preferred such labyrinthine environments. Serpentine routes lent themselves well to his frequent disappearing acts.

From a previous conversation she knew he would not be at home. She had already furnished him with one social lead. Thrilled, he had made plans on the spot to scout around for a modern abstract painting to fit the tastes of the possible client.

It was not, however, quite as easy to pick her way into his apartment. "Paranoid!" she muttered as she put down her tool, useless against the special lock he had installed. A half hour later she had all but risked her life scaling several ledges, jumping to a lower rooftop, and shimmying down a drainpipe. Her last feat consisted of leaping from the metal pipe to the tiny balcony outside Ramon's back window. For her troubles, Ramon received a full Gypsy curse delivered in their native tongue as Angelina slipped into his shoddy fortress. Had she not had the stamina and muscle tone of a prima ballerina, she'd be lying splattered on the pavement.

As she stood in the small living area, looking about, she had to admit to a certain satisfaction. She had outwitted the scoundrel. If only she could be there to see his face when he returned. Ah, wouldn't that be a treat? He'd probably pound a hole clear through the floor, jumping up and down in one of his rages.

It took only a minute to find the clock. Of course, there had been no doubt in her mind that it would be there. Ramon would never have sold such a possession. It was just the sort of treasure he would hoard for himself. An object like that would be considered a talisman by Ramon, a harbinger of finer things to come; the physical reassurance that he was cut out for better things in life.

Gleaming golden on a crate serving as a nightstand, the clock was ticking away beside Ramon's bed. Angelina scooped it up and carefully slipped it into a soft felt bag she had brought along.

It took a couple of minutes more to cover up her tracks. She closed the window and, finding a wrench in one of Ramon's drawers, ripped away the wood from the outside lock, giving the break-in the appearance of an amateur job. The whole operation was concluded in less than seven minutes.

Within the hour Angelina was back in her apartment, taking a long and serious bubble bath to soak away the crime from her psyche. Even so, she had to admit to a certain exhilaration in pulling off her heist. But, this dipping into the underbelly of life also darkened her spirits. It was something she had to do, however; if not for herself, at least for David. She had no illusions that he would applaud her criminal activity— if he even believed her! But she knew how important the clock was to him and to his family. In the present case, it was a clear example of the means justifying the ends.

There was a performance that night. Angelina danced as if she had not a care in the world. Afterward she signed autographs and kissed cheeks and promised that she would be at this party and that. And while she played her part she kept her eye out for one of the gossips who would have David's exact address. She was in luck. The woman she asked knew precisely the house, and even went into a description of its layout. Angelina did not ask for the telephone number. She would appear unannounced, in person.

When the post performance excitement had finally died away, she shut her dressing room door and changed into a white suit, accessorizing it with gold jewelry. Her hair was swept to one side and fastened with an ebony clasp. Knowing David's opinion of her, the implied purity of the outfit gave her at least a superficial dollop of confidence.

The taxi let her off outside his town house. It was midnight and the area was wrapped in nocturnal peace. What she had expected to find, bore out. Looking up, she saw there were still lights shining on the third floor of David's residence. As so many times before, when they were together in that other, long-ago, faraway lifetime, he was up working.

It took some time for him to answer her insistent ring. To say he looked surprised, even shocked, to find her there hardly did justice to his expression.

"I'm sorry for coming so late," Angelina said, remaining outside. "But I thought that under the circumstances any visit would be an unwelcome intrusion. Quite frankly, I just wanted to get this over with as quickly as possible. Then we can both get on with our lives. May I come in? I've something to give you. And to say. It won't take long."

David, still silent, stepped aside for her to pass.

She hesitated, not knowing where he wanted her to go. After all their intimacy, the formality was ludicrous.

"We can talk in here…" He motioned to a room off to the side of the large reception hall. Going ahead, he flicked the wall switch, activating an enormous chandelier in the center of a very formal and most exquisite living room.

Angelina caught him watching her. "Don't worry, David. I'm not here to case the joint. Actually," Angelina said, placing the felt bag on a round inlaid table, "I've come to return something to you."

She gestured to the sack on the table. Having made her presentation, she stepped back.

David walked over and removed the clock from the cloth. Idly examining it, he said, "I suppose I should say thank you. But that seems a little ridiculous, doesn't it?"

"No. Not at all, actually." Angelina moved away, her back to him. Her hands were clenched at her sides. Could he have seen her face at that moment, he would have known she was seething with rage. Suddenly she whirled back, and in a trembling voice, said, "I just want you to know something, then I'll clear out of here. I did not take this from you. It was stolen by my brother, Ramon. Besides that it was just the sort of thing he'd want anyway, I'm sure he took it in retaliation for me not agreeing to go along with a nasty little scheme of his. I had no idea the clock was taken until you told me. Knowing Ramon, I knew it had to have been him. And knowing Ramon, I knew he could never part with such a treasure. So I took it back."

"Stole it back, you mean?"

"Yes, exactly—I stole it. How else would I have gotten it back to you. This morning I employed every refinement of my Gypsy talents. It made me quite sick to do it. Personally, I loathe thieves. It's one of the reasons I fought so long and hard to become a ballerina." She had been tossing out words, rapid fire. Now she paused, and with her eyes filling, said, "I want you to know that I loved you totally and completely. I had no choice but to leave. But that's another story. And I'm sure you don't want to hear it." Without another word, she started for the entrance.

"Tell me," David said.

Angelina stopped. Slowly, she turned back to him. "Why? What possible difference could it make now?"

"It does, that's all." A pause, and then he said, "Because I want to believe."

An hour later Angelina had told David the entire story about her father's failed enterprises, including his dreams for her to break out of the Gypsy's way of life, and the plot into which Ramon had attempted to draw her.

Wearily, she concluded her tale. "So, you see, I really had no choice, did I?"

David had been listening quietly, seated on a divan opposite Angelina. Now he rose from his place and walked to where she sat. Drawing her up, he said nothing, but merely held her close, stroking her hair, her back. "My poor Gypsy...my poor little Gypsy..."

The way he said it, with such tenderness, with such sweetness, the odious word took on the sound of music to Angelina. Tears coursed down her cheeks. She tried to wipe them away. Sniffing, she said, "You say it like it's almost decent."

"Angelina...it's you I love, not your family. Darling, my sweet darling, perhaps it's I who should beg your forgiveness. I must have seemed like a puppet of my family. I gave you that impression. But it's not true. Maybe once it was, but it hasn't been true for some time. I turned this job down. I walked away from it because I didn't trust myself to even be in the same city with you. That's how much I loved you! And the only reason I took the assignment again was because the whole project would have gone down the tubes. Plus, I've come to enjoy the challenge. And thank God I did come here..." He kissed her then, tenderly, without the anger, but within seconds the heat began to spread, and this time Angelina made no effort to stop the flow of passion.

When he carried her up the stairs in his arms, she giggled, partly out of the release of tension and also because every time he kissed her, he began to wobble.

When he undressed her and lay her prone on the bed, the humor had turned into an urgent yearning. He was finally unclothed and lying beside her, his hands rushing like fire over her body. "David...it's been so long...please, hurry."

But he didn't. He tortured her, delaying his own satisfaction as if he thought he were dreaming and did not want it to end.

"Now, David..." Angelina whispered. "Now..." Rising up to him, they exploded together, two cries of exaltation merging, like their bodies, into one voice.

Three days later David, sitting opposite Angelina, at a restaurant, brought out an engagement ring. He placed it on the table halfway between them. Neither of them said anything. Angelina took the box, opened it, and put the ring on her finger. Then David asked the waiter for another bottle of champagne. And that was all. There were some instances when words only detracted.

The decision about the apartment took more time.

"I'd like it if you were here with me," he said one morning while they lay in bed.

A net of panic descended over her. She turned her face to the side, avoiding his eyes. "David, I've always lived in my own place. I can't imagine any other way."

"Even when we're married?" Gently, he drew her chin back around. Smiling, he said, "Okay. Keep your place. But stay with me. It's not like you're giving up any of your precious Gypsy freedom that way. You're just borrowing a bit of my stability."

"Oh, David...I know it's ridiculous. Thank you, thank you..." She kissed his nose playfully, then his eyes, and finally with total seriousness his mouth. He understood. Her Gypsy ways of independence died hard. Rolling fully atop him, she hugged him. Her

heart, bursting with love, needed to express itself physically. The closeness she felt with him was overwhelming sometimes. There were times when she would
suddenly just stop what she was doing and find tears of
joy trickling from her eyes, so full was she with happiness.

The dwelling arrangement, which was, of course,
more psychological than anything else, worked well for
them. Angelina lived full-time with David, and only
periodically returned to her apartment when she felt the
stirrings of insecurity.

It was on a Monday afternoon three weeks after they
had been united that events transpired that led her to
dash back to her apartment. She bolted the doors, took
the telephone off the hook, and completely severed her
relationship to the threat lying in the outside world. Safe
for the moment, she attempted to piece together the
troubling evidence.

She had earned a free weekend during which her roles
had been danced by her understudy, while she and
David had been the guests of a wealthy industrialist at
a magnificent château located a few hours beyond
Paris. Upon arrival, she and David had been greeted by
a scene of hysteria. The man was absolutely frothing,
railing at the police while his heavily tranquilized wife
smiled woozily from a sofa.

Two Ming vases had disappeared from either side of
the mantle. "Two fabulous museum quality Mings!"
To add insult to injury, the man had only recently wired
the vases into a state-of-the-art security system.

As a bystander, David remained calm throughout the
ordeal with the police and insurance inspector. But that
night, as they lay in bed, she could sense the change in

his emotional state. "You're thinking about the exhibit, aren't you?"

"I am, yes."

"You don't have to worry, David."

"I'm just . . . tense."

"Your security system's the best there is. You've said so a thousand times in the last few months! Why, that's been eighty percent of your job, working to make certain that everything's safe." She wondered if her speech was more to convince him or herself.

"There's no such thing as a foolproof system," David said. "As clever as the people are who designed it, there's always another wizard out there who can bypass all the safeguards."

"But not likely," Angelina said, and pressed herself against his side as if to shelter him from all misfortune.

"No. Not likely."

They returned to Paris early that Sunday afternoon, earlier than they had originally planned, their host's emotional state having deteriorated to the point that he, like his wife, required heavy medical sedation.

No sooner had they arrived back at the town house than the call came from the head of the exhibit's security division. David was to come at once. The police had contacted the official only hours before with some rather disturbing news. Over the past several weeks a rash of art heists had occurred in Paris and in the nearby surrounding countryside. They suspected a criminal ring of the highest professional caliber. There were no clues however. The police were baffled by the cleanness, the sheer ingenuity of the thefts. It was suggested that David might want to review the details of each incident; to be forewarned was to be forearmed.

David left immediately. When he returned his mood was subdued. Angelina was already in bed, reading. She rose and greeted him with a kiss. "Come to bed? I want to hear all the gruesome details."

"Soon," he said, and excused himself to make a few more calls from his office. While she waited, her eyes fell upon the papers he had dropped on the bed when they embraced. She had meant only to clear them off the covers, but a casual glance turned to serious scrutiny as she recognized not just one name but another and a third. They were not good friends of hers, but people on the fringe of her social life. All of them were wealthy and sophisticated. And all of them had been robbed.

The following day Angelina did not return to the town house after her morning's ballet class. Instead, going to her apartment, she escaped back into the relative security of the past. She left a message for David that she was called away unexpectedly. Maybe she would be gone a day or longer. He was not to worry.

Now she was there, locked away in her apartment; alone, she might think more clearly. Being alone was how she had survived the world those many years. It was hard enough to take care of herself, but to be responsible for others—for another—opened up whole new channels of potential pain for her. What if she failed this other? What if she were inadvertently responsible for causing misery to this other? What if the robberies were not just committed against a random selection of the rich and famous? Was there a pattern?

When she finally returned to the town house the following evening, David seemed barely aware that she had been gone. He was on the telephone in his office when she popped her head in, expecting a firm lecture on "mutual trust and support" to be delivered her way. Instead he had only just put down the phone when it rang again. After that, she might have been absent altogether. The calls came one after the next.

Giving up after call number six, Angelina waved and made her way to the bedroom. She was in the huge claw-footed bathtub, soaking amid a mountain of pink bubbles, when David suddenly appeared before her.

A glance and she knew there was trouble. Major trouble.

"What?" she asked. She slid up from the froth, on guard.

"Do you realize that at least half of those who were robbed were hit within three days of social engagements given in their homes?"

"I saw the list. I know most of the people were people you and I know, but—"

"Exactly," David said. "People we know. And both you and I were at every single one of those social functions where the robberies took place afterward."

"David," Angelina said, "you're not suggesting that I had anything to do with—"

"My God, no. But still... somewhere in some detail, in some linkage of some name there'll be a clue... And it's imperative that I find it, Angelina. The police were right. Whoever's pulling this stuff is damned brilliant. Capable of causing me more than one night's loss of sleep."

"The Phoenix Diamond," she said. "You don't actually think there's a chance they could get at it."

"It's got the most fail-safe antitheft system ever devised by mankind. But nothing's completely secure. Nothing."

"Our love is, David," Angelina rushed, as if the subject were not the diamond; as if she were defending her life before a packed courtroom.

"Unfortunately our love can't protect the diamond, Angelina."

The next day she visited Ramon at the antique gallery. Ordinarily, whenever she visited the shop, a glad feeling entered her. Zoltan was always cheery, almost always in the midst of charming some well-heeled customer into a fat sale. The place itself was a marvel of aesthetic delight. There were always fresh flowers in vases and the soft refrains of chamber music lilted just beneath the delicate, hushed conversations. Most of the first offerings were consignment pieces, but success had come early—Ramon had an excellent eye for acquisition—and he and Zoltan were able to make some outright purchases of their own to offer for sale.

No one would have suspected the proprietors were two mischievous vagabonds, rather than the urbane sophisticates who spoke with authority on art objects and antiques from every country and any century. A Gypsy was nothing if not a quick study and a resourceful survivor.

But on the morning in question, a glow of satisfaction did not fill Angelina as she drifted to the back of the gallery and into the plush office Ramon had prepared for himself.

"Did you see Zoltan?" Ramon asked with a wide smile as soon as she appeared. "He's got himself an entire new getup from Bond Street. Cost a bloody fortune, as the Brits would say."

"I saw him. He's with a customer. And he does look splendid. And I don't want to waste any more of my time with small talk, Ramon. I simply want you to tell me what you've been up to."

"Why do I have the impression I'm under suspicion for something?"

"Because you are."

"Really? And what have I done? Or I should say, what have I not done."

"Okay, straight out, here's how it stacks up. There's been a whole slew of robberies. Suspiciously, half of them have occurred at the homes of people I know, and out of those people, maybe half were those whose tastes I so gullibly apprised you."

"No!" Ramon gasped. "I can't believe it! And you think . . . you actually think . . . ?" His face grew quite white, and then red splotches appeared to speckle his cheeks. He was almost trembling with indignation when he said defensively, "Why would I want to ruin what we've built up here legitimately? This is the best thing Father and I have ever done. Do you really think I'd do something stupid to jeopardize this? Look!" he said, and quickly pulled out a ledger book, opening it to display the month's cash flow.

Angelina ran her eyes down the columns. "All right, so you're making money."

"A lot of money," Ramon said pridefully.

"Indeed. A lot of money," Angelina said, impressed.

"There. Am I exonerated?"

"You are," Angelina said. "My apologies."

"Well, I can understand your suspicions," Ramon said magnanimously, and rested his arm about her shoulders. "I haven't always been such a good boy. I'll just have to earn your respect."

He walked her to the front door, and she was almost out when he drew her back, saying, "Ah…any new tips for me?"

"Oh, no, not actually." Then she reconsidered and said, "Wait, I did meet someone the other day. A very well-heeled German importer. He's got these darling little jade figurines from the early eighteenth century. Name's Hans Goclig." She quickly riffled through her address book and found his address and number. "You might want to give him a call if you find anything along that line in your wanderings."

And then, having distributed the bait, she was off.

Chapter Fifteen

It took precisely two days for the fish to take the bait. She and David were at a reception in honor of the curator of London's Tate Museum, who had come to Paris to offer his guidance to David on a particularly ticklish bit of international art negotiating, when the news was dropped.

Angelina noted that David's hand jerked slightly when the story was related; other than that, he seemed as serenely in control of his emotions as ever. It was she who came close to dropping her crystal goblet.

"Poor Hans!" exclaimed the matronly woman who seemed to have her finger on the pulse of every social triumph and transgression on the Continent. "He was absolutely felled by the loss. He's collected those little green people since he was a child. Before he came into his fortune, he actually saved up for them. They were like family, those jade figures. And now, all his children—he calls them that—are gone. Stolen! It's too tragic."

That night David did not come to bed. Angelina fell asleep with the light on and a book open, while waiting for him. At three in the morning, she awoke to find him in the kitchen, drinking tea.

"David...don't worry so." She stood in the doorway. Her feet were bare, and her black hair was tousled, cascading to her shoulders, which were naked but for the two thin silk straps of her gown.

With the light shining through the diaphanous peach silk nightgown, David found her a fetching sight. At any other time he would probably have scooped her into his arms and taken her straight to bed. But at the moment his mind was not in sync with his body.

"Don't worry—Angelina, how can I not worry? I've every reason to be out of my mind. Under the circumstances, I don't think imbibing in a little hot tea in my own kitchen is exactly overreacting."

"But you're upset for nothing. The diamond will be safe."

"And there's a pot of gold at the end of every rainbow, a silver lining to every cloud, unicorns exist, and this world will never have another war," he said, and slammed his cup on the counter. "Don't you understand? Where there are madmen and bad men, there's always uncertainty."

Angelina arched one eyebrow. "Oh? Really? I had no idea. I've always been under the impression this is a planet of absolute virtue."

David couldn't help smiling at that. "Sorry. Really." He held his arm out. "Come here, my dangerous little Gypsy. Look into this cup and tell me. What do the leaves say?"

Angelina peered intently at the few tea shavings. Going along with the drama, she spoke in a sultry tone. "Hmm…it's a bit unclear…but, ah, yes, now I see it. If you were to come upstairs, you would find a warm female body waiting for you."

David frowned. "I see, I see…most interesting. And if I didn't go upstairs?"

"Then you would find a warm female body waiting for you in the kitchen," Angelina intoned with the same mysterious edge. "There is one thing for certain in all of this," she added urgently.

"Let me guess. Could it be that there's a warm female body in my future?"

"Ah, you have the gift, too…" Angelina giggled as David scooped her into his arms, kissing her neck.

"Maybe not that, but another one," David said and, hardened, moved against her as he lifted her nightgown. His body was once again in sync with his mind.

There was no chance she was going to let Ramon get away with his thievery. On the other hand, he still was her brother, and she couldn't bring herself to turn him in to the police. For one thing, the scandal would destroy Zoltan. The best way she had of dealing with the situation was to transform Ramon's victories into failures. If she were lucky, he would lose heart. It was bad enough to risk being caught, but to lose what one risked imprisonment for—that would truly be heartbreaking to Ramon. Or so she hoped.

It took some subtle questioning to learn from Zoltan that they had rented a warehouse to hold some of the larger items of furniture that needed refinishing. Actually, he said, they had rented one place earlier on, but had moved on to a much larger place in a good part of

town. It made a far better impression on clients, should
they want to visit the premises for a preview look at
something. Angelina got the address of the first place
which, according to Zoltan, was no longer leased.

When she was positive Ramon was otherwise engaged, she made a visit to the vacated warehouse. It was
locked up, boarded, and seemingly deserted. But instinct told Angelina not to trust first impressions. After considerable effort she discovered an all-but-invisible
entrance camouflaged by lumber and scrap metal.

Her perseverance found its reward. She might have
entered King Tut's tomb, such was the array of splendid objects meeting her eyes upon stepping into Ramon's secret den. A cursory glance at the treasure trove
gave her the impression that Ramon had already managed to fence at least two-thirds of the items stolen. It
took her a moment to locate his latest heist, the jade
figurines. There were fifty of them and she could barely
lift the carton, but her sense of outrage made her strong
enough to carry them out the door.

She trembled, her body in a cold sweat of fear and
anger, until she was safe in her own apartment. To have
been caught with the figurines in her possession! Ah,
wouldn't that have been a scene? Without wasting time
she dialed the police and speaking quickly and anonymously, gave them the location of the warehouse, ap-
prising them of what they would find. When they asked
her name, she said, "Robin Hood," and hung up.

Her next step was to return the figurines. She might
have left them with the rest of the items, but that was
not good enough for her. Ramon might think the tip-off
to the police was just a lucky shot by someone who
might have turned him in out of spite. But to have the
figurines returned another way, would make him more

personally paranoid; perhaps scare him enough to cut out his criminal activity entirely. Whatever, the return of the figurines would be more difficult. A telephone call telling the owner to pick them up at a certain spot could be dangerous. She'd need to leave the figures somewhere and there was always the chance she'd be seen coming or going by someone. In the final analysis, she decided to return them herself in person.

It took only a few telephone calls to learn Hans Goclig, the owner of the figurines, was to be a guest at a party she and David were scheduled to attend. On the night of the occasion she made herself particularly visible, mingling with everyone, including Hans. She even spoke to him about the theft. How could it have happened? Didn't he have security? It took five minutes of conversation for her to have a complete understanding of his security system, plus a general idea of the layout of his house.

A half hour later, she complained of a raging headache and insisted that David stay while she went home to rest. An hour later, Angelina had managed to replace the figurines.

She had only just slipped into bed when David arrived home.

"You're not going to believe this," he said excitedly.

Angelina lifted her head off the pillow, squinting as if still suffering from the ache in her noggin. "Believe what, darling?"

"You know those jade figurines? The ones that were stolen recently."

"Hmm...oh, yes...vaguely."

"They were returned. The call came while I was at the party. One of the servants reported them found in a box, sitting on the kitchen counter." David undressed as he spoke. His fingers moved rapidly, unfastening diamond studs.

"Returned? How extraordinary," Angelina said.

"Weird, is more like it."

"Extraordinarily weird. Well, whatever, at least there's a happy ending to it all. Come to bed, David . . . my headache seems to have suddenly lifted."

The news was in the papers the next day, both about the tip-off on the warehouse treasure trove, and the jade figures mysteriously showing up at the owner's residence.

Angelina made it a point to invite Zoltan and Ramon for lunch. Zoltan was the one to bring up the news item. Ramon on the other hand, remained mute on the subject.

"Ramon, is something wrong? You seem unusually silent this day," Angelina commented. "More bread?"

"I have things on my mind." He looked across the table at her, his expression darker than she had ever before noted. But he took the basket of bread.

As for David, he seemed in an almost jubilant mood that evening. "I feel like a weight's been lifted somehow," he explained over their late supper.

"How's that?" Angelina inquired, sipping from her wineglass.

"Well, the police are analyzing the whole thing. They've got something to go on finally. If they're lucky, they may trace the gang that pulled off these jobs. With any luck, they'll be out of business before the exhibition."

"That is good news," Angelina said, hoping to God she had wiped off all her own prints and covered all tracks that might lead to her own doorway.

Two days later another theft was reported, this time of a fabulous Chinese ivory horse. And the following night, amazingly, the horse returned home to graze on its rosewood stand from which it had been pilfered.

"Do you think these little figures are maybe somehow taking life on their own?" Angelina asked, laughing, after David recounted the details of the latest bewildering theft, even before it hit the papers. "The jade people just took off on a caper to see the city, then decided home was the best place to be after all. And the horse may have gotten tired of munching on rosewood—went in search of the real green stuff."

David laughed with her. "It's a thought," he said. "I'll mention it to the police."

Within the next two and a half weeks, five separate robberies occurred and two returns were made of the pilfered objects. The newspapers were having a field day over the situation. From the police report they had first adopted the "Robin Hood" angle, but because the informant was a woman, decided that "Maid Marion" was an even more romantic tag on which they might capitalize. Speculations abounded as to what was going on in the theft/returns.

As for Angelina, her nerves were positively frayed. For one thing, there was always the chance that she might be caught in one of her daring "Marion" escapades. That would really help David's credibility as the protector of the Phoenix Diamond, wouldn't it? The donors would probably pull it from the exhibition, and justifiably so.

The other great difficulty she faced was simply the time factors with which she had to contend. She was constantly on the go. First she had to keep close tabs on Ramon, to figure out where his latest hiding place was located. This she did through consulting Zoltan as to Ramon's habits and sometimes through following her brother.

Then she had to arrange for time away from her dance schedule, from her social life with David, and from her personal life. She had used headaches, interviews that never materialized, shopping, a meeting with an old, nonexistent girlfriend, anything and everything to buy herself freedom to accomplish her task.

She was, in a word, exhausted.

"What's this?" David asked her one day when she had returned later than expected from a bogus shopping spree.

Angelina had just come out of the bath. Still pink from the hot water, she felt a chill as David seemed to look past her body and into the borderline hysteria of her mind.

David was holding up a strange looking outfit. It was, Angelina saw, a skirt and sweater set, in as putrid a shade of mustard as ever existed. She had been so crazy from her last exploit of replacing a Fabergé egg, which she had almost dropped, that she had given no thought at all to the purchase that she made afterward. She'd grabbed the first thing she saw in the store, needing something to bring home as proof of her whereabouts.

"Oh, that? It's for my friend. She's one of the few women I've ever known who can wear that color."

"The friend I've never met?" asked David.

He was still looking at her curiously when she crossed the room and took the outfit from his hands. "She's so busy lately. You know journalists . . . tight deadlines."

"Angelina?"

"Yes, David?" She used every ounce of her willpower to meet his gaze squarely.

"What is going on with you?"

"Nothing, darling. Let's go to bed—"

David caught her by the arm, and swung her around to him. "No. Let's not go to bed. You've used that device too many times during the past few weeks. I'm not so dumb that my brains get completely scrambled by your body, love."

"Are you accusing me of something? Of some...infidelity, David? Is that it? Do you think I'm running around on you? Having a wild affair with someone?"

"I'll admit, the idea did occur to me."

"And?"

"And I rejected it."

"Well, thank you very much."

"Look at you. You're an absolute basket case. I love you...don't you understand that? When I see you like this, it worries me. There's got to be a reason and I'd like to know what it is."

"All right. It's Sasha," she lied, knowing she had to come up with something plausible.

"Sasha? What's the matter with Sasha?"

"Oh, he's always pushing me. He wants so much out of me. And then we fight. We both demand perfection, you know. Sometimes I have trouble living up to my ideal of how I should be, how the world should be. I want everything exactly right." That at least was the truth.

"Well maybe you should take a more realistic look at what really matters in your life."

"Yes," she said, "that's what I should do. I really should. David...you're absolutely right."

That night Angelina lay in bed thinking that she, in fact, did have to make some decisions based upon reality. She physically could not continue on her present path of living a dual existence. She was trying to protect Zoltan long enough for Ramon to be forced out of business on his own, without bringing in the police and the ensuing scandal. Any ugly publicity would cripple Zoltan's last chance at respectability, not to mention what the news would do to David's image. She had thought that Ramon would give up by now; instead he had even stepped up his rash of thefts! It had been weeks since she had supplied him with any real information on friends she knew. Ramon was on his own now, and running wild. Somehow the whole thing had to come to a stop. And fast.

The next morning she was so exhausted she could barely lift her body out of bed to wash her face. She dreaded reading the newspaper, for fear of what she would find. David had placed it on her nightstand, along with a cup of café au lait. Angelina slipped back beneath the covers and, with a sense of doom, pulled the paper before her.

David, almost finished dressing, watched her from across the room. "There's been another one."

Through the thick fringe of her lashes, Angelina could see she was being carefully observed. "Another robbery?"

"A jewel this time," David said. His voice was tight.

"Oh?" Angelina felt a knot form in her stomach. Her mind turned instantly to the Phoenix Diamond. That bloody Ramon would not be so stupid to think that...oh, but Ramon's arrogance knew no bounds! Perhaps that was how he had managed to be so successful for so long. Audacity carried him half the way. Truly Ramon tread where the most intrepid of angels feared to set foot. *That damn Ramon!* Now he was going too far.

As it turned out, it was Ramon who made the decisive move in ending the cat and mouse game they had been playing.

As on other occasions, directly after one of the thefts, Angelina appeared at the antique shop ostensibly to speak with Zoltan. A question here, an answer there, and Zoltan gave her the information she required to trace down the jewel's whereabouts. She also learned that Ramon had flown to Geneva that morning to consult with a banker about an estate sale. With her mind in turmoil, she remained a few minutes more to listen to Zoltan rhapsodize over the shop's success.

"It has given me the status I needed," he confided in Angelina. "My people once again look up to me. With the money I am making here, I am starting to give out small loans to help them with their own legitimate businesses."

"I'm glad," Angelina said wearily. She was happy for him, but to deliver more enthusiasm would have probably drained her of the little strength she had left. "At last, you've gotten the life you've always wanted."

"Yes...yes..." Zoltan agreed. "But..." His eyes took on a faraway look.

Angelina waited. "But?"

"Umm, sometimes...well, the old ways...they had a certain, uh, edge. You know?"

"Like getting sliced in two by the edge of a knife, I'd say."

"Yes, that is true. Nevertheless...ah, a customer!"

And Zoltan was off to make more money—legitimately.

Angelina also had things to do. A moment later, in the back of a taxi, she sat brooding, wondering how the hell she was going to get this latest of objects back into the hands of its owner.

Ten minutes later she was deposited at an address on the Rue de Mouffetard. Being before twelve, the street was teeming with people shopping the outdoor markets. The place she sought was directly next to a condemned inelegant eighteenth century building. It looked in as sad a state as its neighbor, although apparently it had managed to survive the architectural death warrant.

Angelina picked her way through a courtyard of debris and past a doorway dangling at angle from its rusted hinges into the interior. As she moved stealthily through the various rooms, searching for the place where Ramon might have hidden his stash, she felt a growing sense of apprehension. She shook it off as being no more than extreme tiredness and continued on.

But at the top floor, her fear was explained.

"Hello, Angelina."

Chapter Sixteen

David was half out the front door when he remembered he had to call a friend. It was too important a call to put off. He had to arrange a meeting with a member on the Getty Museum's board of directors. As he was already downstairs, and therefore close to the dainty cherrywood secretary in which Angelina kept her address directory, he thought to use it rather than climb back up the stairs to get the number from his office.

He was really in a hurry, and was peeved when locating it didn't turn out to be quite the easy matter he had anticipated. Finally he found the book. It was wedged beneath some papers in the back of the middle drawer. He was scanning for his party's listing when the brief penciled notations beside various names caught his attention.

The inscriptions seemed to represent some kind of a code. Momentarily intrigued, he played a quick game with himself, trying to figure out the meanings. At first it seemed a hopeless endeavor and he was about to scratch the enterprise and get on with his business when something struck him. The initials "CH.M.D.V." suddenly transposed themselves into "Chinese Ming Dynasty Vases." With a feeling of foreboding he continued to decipher other groupings of letters, and within three or four minutes had unraveled the code.

He didn't want to pursue what he had stumbled upon, but once begun he couldn't turn away from his discovery. There was too much at stake for too many people other than himself. It would be unconscionable to stick his head in the sand, regardless of his personal feelings.

With fingers close to trembling, he lifted his briefcase to the desk and opened it. He removed the folder containing information on the art heists supplied to him by the police. Given his various dealings in the art field, they had thought he might stumble upon some stray detail that would lead to solving the mysterious crimes.

The names of the victims were there in a neat computer printout. Beside each name was a note of the item stolen. In each case, the information correlated to the coded entries in Angelina's address book.

At no other time in his life had he been filled with such despair as at that moment. Even when Angelina had walked out on him in New York, deep within his heart he had somehow always held to the belief that she had cared about him, that there was something to explain her disappearance other than lack of feeling.

But now, this evidence belied all the trust they had established between them during the past months.

Questions without answers raced through David's mind. Was it possible that she had only reunited with him to have closer access to the Phoenix Diamond? The investigator's warnings echoed in his mind. *A Gypsy is a Gypsy right through to her genes. A Gypsy can't be rehabilitated. Once a thief, always a thief.*

David had thought otherwise, and when they were reunited he was convinced of Angelina's sincerity when she insisted she had abandoned all allegiance to her family's ways.

But here was proof to the contrary.

Could he have been such a fool? He did not consider himself to be a stupid man. True, he had a soft spot or two, but no one could say he was ordinarily gullible. But his instincts were split between trust of the woman he loved and bowing to suspicions based upon empirical evidence. He shoved the book back into the drawer, thinking now that there had been a good reason for it being hard to locate.

His guts churned as he stepped, briefcase in hand, into the hall, just as Angelina came running down the stairs.

She seemed surprised to find him still there, and for a moment stopped in her journey. "Oh, David ... I'd thought you'd already left."

"Just on my way out. Had to make a call." He studied her face, even as she appeared to be examining him in the same intense manner. He was always having to remind himself that the woman he loved was not only beautiful and talented, but had a mind that worked with the efficiency of a computer. Plus, she had that strange sixth sense. "Off somewhere?"

"Yes ... thought I'd meet Susan for breakfast. With her tight schedule, she barely has time for me anymore. Breakfast's the only chance really. So, I'm just off."

"Ah, well give Susan my regards, and tell her I'm looking forward to meeting her."

"I will, I will . . ." Angelina said, bounding down the stairs.

"Would you like a lift?" He held his breath, hoping against hope that she would say yes and that the whole issue of her duplicity would be resolved in that one ride.

"Thanks, but no. I've already called a cab." She gave him a quick kiss as she flew out the door.

David waited only a moment before leaving himself. As he locked the door, he saw the taxi pull slowly up and Angelina climb in. David's own car was at the curb waiting for him. The uniformed driver quickly opened the back passenger door.

"Gaston," David said, seating himself in the vehicle's back, "I've forgotten to give Ms. Zarsuela something. It's very important. Just follow that cab she's taken. I'll catch up with her."

David hated himself for what he was doing—for what he *had* to do.

The chain of coincidences had turned to suspicions, which had hardened into what was now almost incontestable evidence that Angelina was in some way, directly or indirectly, involved with the rash of burglaries.

There were too many loose threads and unexplained antics for him not to take some sort of conclusive action to end the mystery that plagued his mind night and day. He simply had to know what was going on. Spying on her . . . well, it was odious . . . but he had no other choice, unless he were to call in the police. Unthinkable.

A few minutes later, it came as no surprise to find that Angelina had been let off at her father's antique store, rather than going to breakfast with the undoubtedly fictional Susan. But, even so, giving her the benefit of the doubt, he changed cars and waited in a taxi to see if her next step might be to rendezvous with her mysterious journalist friend.

Moments later, Angelina reappeared and hailed another cab. They were off again.

David followed her to the Rue de Mouffetard. There he saw her leave the cab and make her way unsurely into a decrepit building. No matter how bohemian Susan might be, it was inconceivable that she or anyone else could live in such a place.

David paid the cab driver and got out, making certain to stay out of sight.

At first he was going to follow her into the rubbled structure, but at the last moment backed down. He was without the heart for such a dramatic confrontation. What he would do was wait for her to exit. Then, in a bid to be rational and civilized, he would suggest they go someplace where the truth might be at last exchanged.

"So, it was you, little sister," Ramon said, moving slowly toward Angelina.

"Shouldn't that be my line?"

"How long did it take you to put things together?"

"Long enough."

"Well, I'll admit it took me a while to figure out you were the one messing things up for me. But who else could it have been? Who else would have had the nerve? Only another Zarsuela. We *are* the best, aren't we?"

"You have a perverted sense of family pride."

"Well, anyway, I've been expecting you. Zoltan must have given you the same right information he's been feeding you all along. Only this time it was information I wanted you to have."

Ramon stood almost nose to nose with her. Angelina held her ground, if for no other reason than she was too stunned for a moment to move from the spot.

The upstairs room of the abandoned building was obviously inhabited at times by large rats, the largest of which was now her brother. Sunlight filtered through the latticed shutters, painting stripes over Ramon's face.

"You've come for this, I believe," Ramon said. He opened his palm to display the gem taken the night before.

"You're not going to get away with this anymore, Ramon."

"Oh, really?"

"Yes, really. I tried to stop you the easy way. I thought I'd give you a lesson in crime not paying. But apparently you're a slow learner."

"Look, little sister, let me explain some facts of life to you. First of all, I am not necessarily the monster you would have me be. I *did* try to make a go of things the honest way—your way. But it was too slow. We didn't have the right stock and we had no money to get it. It's not as if there's no competition in this city. Other dealers have family connections. They have . . . well, what difference does it make? I just used the resources of my own family to best advantage. I used my experience. That's all I've been given in life, Angelina. A complete education in thievery and running and—"

"Yes, I know all of that. So spare me. Either you stop this at once, or the next time you pull one of your midnight unauthorized requisitions, I'm turning you in to the police."

"No you won't. And here's why. Because if you do, I will turn you in to the police. I've got all the information you've given me about your hotsy-totsy friends neatly listed in notebooks."

"I only gave you information on what things they liked based upon what they've collected in the past. That hardly constitutes being an accessory to a crime, Ramon."

"True. But, you see, I've put it down a little differently. I've recorded what things they own and even the floor plans of their houses. I'll merely tell the police it was all furnished by you. Do you think they'll believe you're innocent? A Gypsy? No, you'll not be running to the police, love.

"Now, there's something else." Ramon stepped away and began to drift through the room, gesturing as if he spoke before an audience. "This Phoenix Diamond. This could change everything in one fell swoop—for Zoltan and for me. This could make us rich enough to retire from any kind of business forever. I want that stone, Angelina." His eyes bore into her with all the intense fire of his conviction.

She laughed. "Isn't the Phoenix Diamond just a slight jump out of your league, Ramon? You wouldn't even have the sources to unload it."

"Yes, well, I've already researched that," he said. "The disposal of that diamond will be handled. Now, then, you—" he pointed to her "—you have something to do in this. You're to get me the blueprints of the security system surrounding the diamond. When you do, I promise—really promise this time—you will never see me involved in another illegal enterprise."

"No," Angelina said coldly. "I refuse to lift one finger to help you."

Ramon stared at her for a long moment, obviously surprised he had not bullied her into submission. "Fine," he said at last. "Then I'll inform the police of your part in the unfortunate thefts. Anonymously, of course. Zoltan will have no future. You will be ruined professionally and socially, not to mention what the news will do to your darling David when he learns that the only reason you returned to him was to get closer to the diamond. And David's career will, no doubt, suffer a considerable downturn as well." Ramon paused to enable her to digest all that he had spoken. "So, Angelina, think again. What's it to be?"

"Forget it, Ramon. Forget your threats. The answer's no, still no, forever no. You'll get no help from me."

Ramon merely stared at her in disbelief. "Are you crazy?" he asked finally.

"Don't you see, David's the only thing I care about? In your lousy scheme, David gets the short end of the stick, no matter what."

"But what about Zoltan? And you'd be throwing away your entire future."

"Of course I care about Zoltan. But he's taken care of himself this long. I'll just have to pray he survives his son's treachery. And as for me . . . physically and emotionally, I can't continue living a double life. You do what you have to do. I'll do what I have to do."

Ramon nodded. "Well, at least we understand each other. If you change your mind, let me know before it's too late."

Ramon left, walking past her without another word. Left alone, Angelina studied his footprints left in the dust. That was what her life would be soon: dust.

* * *

David was positioned by a stand selling apples. He was watching when the figure came bounding out of the building's entrance. It was not Angelina, but there was little doubt about the man's identity. It had to be Ramon, Angelina's brother. Her description had been chillingly accurate; he was a compelling presence, darkly handsome, dressed in the latest fashion, and in many ways a masculine version of his beautiful sister.

So, there it was, David thought. He would have to accept the facts: there could be no other reason for Angelina to have met with Ramon in such quarters unless it was for nefarious purposes; unless Angelina was in league with Ramon. It was all but impossible to believe, but the bad seed had finally found fertile ground and taken root in Angelina.

That night, David took the call from their bedroom. As he spoke, he surreptitiously watched Angelina, who was dressing for a formal dinner party they were to attend in an hour. "Excellent, excellent!" David commented. "Then I should be at the airport to greet the Phoenix contingent on Friday? Well, yes, the press is a necessary evil. As long as the security measures go as planned, there won't be any trouble. And the system at the museum will be activated tomorrow. Let's keep our fingers crossed."

"The diamond's coming in on Friday?" Angelina asked.

She slipped a beaded cobalt-blue gown over her head. Like a blue waterfall, the dress fell softly over her body. Her hair was worn long and full to her shoulders. At her ears were the new blue sapphire and diamond earrings he had given her.

To David, that was the biggest puzzle of all. He could afford to give her damn near anything she wanted. And that was something else strange. Whereas she always seemed to appreciate and approve of the gifts he gave her, she never actually suggested any of them. It wasn't as if she were hinting for a new diamond necklace or even a painting. Hell! He would have bought her a hundred jade Chinese figurines, if that would have pleased her. So why? Why did she have to go to such lengths to own things that she might have legally enjoyed? It didn't make sense.

"You don't seem to understand, Mr. Winthrop. Thieving is in their blood."

Well, now he would have to understand. He owed that much, at least, to the people who had entrusted him with the safety of some of the world's greatest art treasures. As for the Phoenix Diamond, God help them all if something happened to it. A holy war was not too difficult to envision.

"Yes," David finally answered, having pretended involvement with his diamond studs, "believe it or not, the diamond will finally be arriving on Friday."

"Under heavy guard, I suppose?"

David cast her a quick look. "The heaviest," he assured her. "I doubt if even the Crown Jewels of England have an edge on our security."

"That's a relief," Angelina said. She sat down at her dressing table to check her makeup. Then she swiveled around on the stool. A frown creased her brow and there was worry in the dark eyes. "Oh, David...I know you've enjoyed putting together this whole thing, but really, I'll be so happy when it's over. It makes me nervous."

"Don't worry. Everything has been done to ensure the safety of the exhibit. Particularly the diamond."

"Then you don't think there's the slightest chance that it might be stolen?"

"None, absolutely no chance at all. The thief would find it the worst move of his career."

Angelina was quiet for a moment, then in a casual tone, as she turned back to the mirror, she said, "Would it be totally out of the question for me to get a peek at the security diagrams?"

"What on earth for?" David responded just as easily, although his gut had tightened. He felt the tiny ray of hope he had nurtured begin to shrivel.

"Well," she said, rising and walking toward him with a sheepish, and as always, beautiful smile. "I know this sounds very strange. But you know my family's, uh, shall we say, line of work. I've been privy to every kind of break and entry trick in the book, and a whole lot more that weren't ever recorded."

"These are highly sophisticated plans, Angelina."

"Gypsies are highly sophisticated in certain areas. It's instinctive. They may not have degrees from M.I.T., but they have ways of working around any kind of barrier. They're motivated when they want something." She kissed him, her tongue probing his languorously, her body insinuating in its rhythm.

David tightened his hold on her, but not out of passion. He closed his eyes, begging whatever god or gods existed in the universe to help him, to help her, to intervene in the name of love!

"You really want to see the plans?"

"Yes, yes I do . . ." Angelina said.

David searched her eyes, inwardly pleading with her to reverse this crazy desire, to prove him wrong. "Okay. Okay, Angelina. If this is what you really want. Give me a day, maybe two. I'll get a copy for you."

Chapter Seventeen

They were secret plans; doubly secret because they were not the real plans. David had had duplicates made of the authentic diagrams, and then had those doctored by an expert. Anyone who used those plans would literally be sealing his own fate. An attempt on the diamond would instantly close off all entrances to the exhibition room, and at the same time summon both inside security guards plus the police.

David placed the schematics neatly on Angelina's dressing table, where she would find them after her morning bath. By then he would be gone and whatever happened after, well, that was up to her. The thought, as well as the act, seemed horribly callous.

Regardless, what could he do about anything? That was the misery of the situation.

He had thought long and hard about what course he should take. In the end, he decided he had no other

choice than to follow through on his promise to supply
Angelina with the plans she had requested. He did not
think of himself as brave, nor as decisive. He would
settle for prudent.

No matter what, he could not be the one to turn her
in to the police. There was still the slightest hope, the
barest thread of a chance that she might have a turn of
heart. Even at the twelfth hour, she could still recon-
sider and abandon her scheme. Couldn't she see it for
what it was? It was a futile enterprise, doomed to fail-
ure.

No, David thought as he walked from the bedroom,
he could do nothing overt to foil her plans. No matter
what she had done, he loved her enough to give her this
last opportunity to rethink her future—their future. If
the decision did not come from her, there would be
nothing for them anyway.

It had become a custom to lunch with Zoltan at least
once a week, just the two of them, father and daughter. Angelina took advantage of their established social
engagement to meet with Zoltan without arousing Ramon's suspicious nature.

"I've got something to show you," Angelina said to
her father when they were finished with dessert. She
handed him the diagrams David had left for her that
morning. Zoltan unfurled them. He spread them out at
an angle and studied them with interest.

"Umm..." he said finally. He also nodded appre-
ciatively.

"What, umm?" Angelina was beside herself with
apprehension. Her relationship to the diagrams was as
a bumpy truck to a vial of nitroglycerin. Mishandled,
everything in her life would explode.

"Very interesting." Zoltan looked up. A twinkle had taken residence behind his eyes. "Security plans for the art exhibit."

It wasn't a question, but a fact. Angelina nodded anyway, as if he had asked. "I want to know if they're any good. I mean, do you think they're absolutely invulnerable to theft?"

"Ah, this I cannot say for sure." Zoltan shrugged, and again looked down to appraise the prints. "These are very complicated," he said. "They would require some study. Leave them with me and—"

Angelina scowled. Her voice held disappointment. "No, I can't. I mean, David would only suspect the worst. I don't want to add to his load of worries. I've got to return them by tonight."

"We can make copies," Zoltan said. "Come, we will make use of electronic magic."

"And then you'll be able to tell me if there are any holes in the system?"

"If there are holes, I will find them. Or, I am not Zoltan, king of my people. On the other hand . . ." He winked, and leaned in closer. "I am not usually on the side of the good guys, either."

Angelina followed as Zoltan swaggered from the restaurant, his hands literally holding David's future.

After the copies were made and she had extracted Zoltan's most solemn promise that he would let no one see the plans, she returned home with the originals.

Late that afternoon David returned early. He found her curled in a chair in their bedroom, the plans open in her lap.

"Well?" he asked, coming up and kissing her lightly on the forehead before going off to loosen his tie and undo his shirt. "Is the diamond safe?"

Angelina let the plans lie in her lap and, running her fingers through her hair, said in consternation, "To be honest, I can't tell. It's beyond me, all these lines and, well...it all looks very professional and complicated. But..." And here she stopped.

"But?" David swiveled slowly around, studying her face for signs of remorse, hints of treachery.

"I don't know," Angelina said, seeming to recede into a part of herself off bounds from him. She rolled up the drawings. "I just have this feeling."

"A feeling, you say?" David kept the tone casual. It was an effort. What ploy was this? Was it some sort of clever groundwork she was laying for what would happen in the future? God, he thought, the infernal, never ending questions...

"Yes. It's...well, it's stupid. But I just don't get a good feeling from holding these. There's something...wrong. David, are you satisfied the security system is absolutely safe?"

"Absolutely," he returned. Her concern appeared so genuine, he was almost touched. He might almost believe she was truly worried for him. But, no, he knew better. He knew entirely too much about his beautiful lover to be so trusting. "These drawings absolutely guarantee the safety of the diamond," he finished, the irony leaving a bitter taste in his mouth.

Ramon was with a customer when Zoltan returned. He immediately sensed a change in his father. There was something of the old Gypsy spirit in his walk, and the light in his eye was too wicked not to prompt a second glance, a second thought, and eventually, a closer inspection of the cause. Something was up.

Ramon's initial suspicions were further bolstered when Zoltan spent considerable time that afternoon locked in his office. An hour or two after closing time, Zoltan was still hiding away. Ramon had knocked several times, on various pretenses, but each time had been shooed away. Now he hovered outside the door, trembling with curiosity to know what absorbed his father.

Finally, at Ramon's insistent urging, Zoltan sprang the lock, permitting the door to open a mere crack. "Yes, yes! Do you never take a hint, Ramon?"

"Never. At least not when I'm after something." An eye, a nose, part of Zoltan's mouth; this was all the view Ramon got for his efforts.

"What do you want?" Zoltan asked gruffly.

Ramon could tell Zoltan could hardly wait to get back to whatever-it-was. Infuriated that he couldn't have access to the "thing", but hiding his emotions, Ramon gave a push against the door, as if he had not noted the inhospitality. To camouflage his fervor, he kept up a running babble. "A client told me of a wonderful place to eat. The woman's fat as can be. That's a good recommendation, what? She ought to know food."

He did not succeed in clearing a path. Zoltan's arm came up too soon. His foot wedged in between the door and the frame, curtailing Ramon's progress.

"On the other hand," Zoltan said, "maybe she is indiscriminate. Maybe she only stuffs her face with junk food."

Ramon grunted. His mind was on his mission, which hadn't gone too well. His only reward was a bit more space in which to examine the interior of the office. At least it was something. With the door only partially ajar, Ramon had to crane his neck to peer beyond his father's form.

What his glance took in all but took his breath away. Spread out on the desk, drawings of conduits and the paths of laser beams and . . . oh, it was all too fantastic! Fate had smiled on him!

He swallowed, and with an easy smile backed slightly away, not to arouse any suspicion, "Anyway, I thought a nice pepper steak?" He made what he considered an inviting smacking noise with his lips.

Zoltan agreed, as Ramon pretty much assumed he would. He would have laid money down on it. In a world of uncertainties, there were few absolute guarantees, but this was one of them: a good steak was high on Zoltan's list of irresistible temptations.

A salad, a pepper steak, some french fries later, all washed down by two bottles of a fine cabernet—and Ramon had Zoltan's spirits sailing with the moon. Dutifully, Ramon insisted on seeing Zoltan to his apartment, personally checking to make certain he locked himself in for a good sound sleep.

And then Ramon tore back to the antique store.

A mere jimmy and pick later, he was in Zoltan's office rifling through his desk, finally to discover what he sought in a secret compartment on the underside of a side drawer.

Almost hyperventilating from excitement, Ramon spread the plans out before him. "Ah . . ." he said. "Thank you very much little sister." He should have known she would consult Zoltan. At one time Zoltan had, arguably, been the best in Europe when it came to breaking and entering through complex mechanized security systems. No doubt he had fallen behind on the latest equipment, but he still had a larcenous mind, and a trickster's mind would always carry him further than any typical man's education. Too bad, Ramon thought, that Zoltan's body, thickened over the years, could no longer dart and dodge as it once had. Zoltan had been so splendid as a thief. In fact, Zoltan had taught him everything.

Ramon retrieved his camera from his own office and took several shots of each page, just to be on the safe side. Next, he took care to replace the rolled plans exactly as he had found them, relocked the door, and scurried off in search of an all-night developing studio.

There was little time to spare. The Phoenix Diamond would be in place in less than two days. In place, that is, for a brief time...

It was David's night.

Angelina stood proudly by his side as they greeted men and women with social and economic pedigrees as long as the reception line. They were in the Grand Ballroom of the hotel. A conservative estimate seemed to establish at least fifteen hundred guests in attendance. Seemingly, everyone who was anyone in the cultural establishment was there to celebrate David's glorious accomplishment of uniting countries from all over the world in one immense, cooperative undertaking.

"This is embarrassing," Angelina whispered as the invitees to the opening filed past, each person smiling and commenting upon the success of the exhibition. "And sticky. Must they kiss my hand? And all that bowing...oh, David, it's really too much."

"It's when they fling themselves prostrate at my feet that annoys me. Hard on the arches," David commented from the side of his mouth as he shook hands with a young Japanese prince.

"On the other hand, maybe they're just after your shoes. They certainly cost enough to be worth a lunge."

Angelina had chosen her own outfit from a Parisian design house. More costly than anything she had ever owned, it was a dark wine color, inlaid with seed pearls and semiprecious stones, in truth, a dress certainly fit for a queen. Her hair was worn up, displaying the ruby and pearl earrings David had designed himself for the outfit.

The exhibition's opening night was a gala for the press and those individuals and organizations who had generously contributed time and money, social connections, and in some cases, the artwork, itself. The rank and file public would stroll past beginning the following morning. Tickets had been on sale for the past two months, and there was talk of extending the exhibition to accommodate the vast demand by the public.

The feeling came over Angelina all at once, unbidden and unexpected. Standing beside David, who was smiling and saying something to a Spanish couple, Angelina experienced a flood of emotion so warm and full and complete for him that its very intensity seemed to set up a vibration in every cell and nerve ending in her body.

The moment existed out of time, in its own space and its own reality. For that instant, she swam in an ocean of love.

Then the man appeared at David's side. He was young and somber and dressed in a blue blazer with Security imprinted on a plastic badge. He talked in a rush. "Excuse me, Mr. Winthrop...something, something... I think you'd better come at once."

It was the man's voice, rather than his message, that turned Angelina's world of bliss to one of terror.

"David?" She placed her hand on his arm, but when he looked at her his eyes belonged to a stranger, someone she didn't know, who seemed to take offense at the misplaced intimacy.

Without a word, he turned from her and followed the security guard from the room. Angelina watched after him, a numbing cold having replaced the warmth of only a moment before. Someone was speaking to her, the reception line David had just left, having continued on.

"Sorry...excuse me," Angelina said, also abandoning her position as official greeter.

The news was given just as she reached David in the lobby.

"A break-in at the exhibition. It's in the Phoenix room, I'm afraid. Sorry, sir," the guard said, "...the diamond..."

"Oh, David..." she began, her heart exploding in grief and terror. Grasping hold of his arm, she wasn't sure if it was to save herself from falling or to support David, who had turned to face her.

His face was a stark white, washed clean of its usual high color. Shards of desperate pain radiated outward from his eyes. He spoke to her in a voice low and urgent. Seeming distant and impassioned at the same instant, he formed impossible words. "Angelina... Angelina...what have you done?"

"I haven't done anything. David...David, I've done nothing. What do you think?" she cried, and even as she defended herself against the unknown crime, the agony in his face intensified.

"Listen to me." He drew her away from anyone who might hear. "There's time for you to get out now. Sooner or later the police will discover the truth, just as

I did. Oh, damn, Angelina!'' He grabbed her by the shoulders, then thrust her away, as if to save himself of some ultimate contamination. "I loved you. Loved you. I left this all up to you. It was your decision. Either you wanted the diamond or you wanted me. You couldn't have both, so you chose. And now you have to live with that choice. Unfortunately, so do I.'' He felt inside his jacket, and from an inside pocket withdrew an envelope. "There's a ticket in here. One way to South America. And there's money in the envelope. That's all the help I can give you, and God knows if I really ought to be giving you that."

A terrible pain rose up in Angelina, a pain as eternal and full as her love had been only a moment before. Her hand swept back and then forward, whipping against David's face. "You bastard! You thought I—you think that I—'' Tears came in torrents, garbling her words, making her gasp to catch her breath. An ugly, mocking red mark formed on his face. That their love, their sweetness should come to this hate-filled brawl! Too much...too much to bear...she would die from this moment...die a million times, over and over again. "All this time you've been thinking that I was a liar! A thief! A cheat! I was loving you, and you thought that of me? Well, there was a lie, all right. Our whole relationship's been a lie from start to finish."

"I didn't want to see the things I saw. I didn't want to know what I found out. But I did, Angelina. And no matter how much I love you, I can't be a party to your way of life. Take the ticket and get out of here while you can.'' When she didn't accept his offering, he turned and walked quickly through the hotel lobby to the front entrance.

Angelina dashed after him. He was outside by the time she caught up with him.

"David! I want to go, too! You're wrong. I had nothing to do with this. I'll show you...prove to you..."

He turned briefly. His eyes were wild, not just with the panic of the situation, but brimming with revulsion and fury, and most of all with an abject, paralyzing sorrow.

It was only just a glance, but it stunned her as if some violence had been committed. Then he turned from her and made hasty arrangements for his car to be brought around.

Angelina could only stand there, speechless and defenseless, for once in her life unable to react. Everything was happening so fast. There were other people there now, members of the art committee who had somehow gotten wind of the exhibition break-in, and who now clamored for assurance that there was no truth to the hideous rumor being circulated.

She could hear David's voice, breaking in and out above the roar. He was telling them not to jump to conclusions.

It might have been a war. It might have been the end of the world and some last impulse to survive stirred in her. She had to get to him, to make things right.

Fighting her way every inch, she reached David, who was stepping into his car just as she made it to his side.

"David!" she shouted. "Wait! Let me come, too."

When his eyes met hers, it was as if she were being stabbed. And when he spoke, the knife was twisted, again and again. "Damn you, Angelina! Damn you," he said under his breath. "We had everything, and you had to throw it all away for some lousy stone."

"No...David...please..." But the door slammed closed. She was dismissed, shut out of his life.

The private limousine sped forward. Around her, bodies swirled and jostled and milled and crushed. She was drowning, drowning in the sea of pandemonium. "What's happened?" she suddenly screamed aloud.

She was beseeching God, but instead a man turned to her, and with his eyes enflamed, said in a sputtering voice, "I've got my Degas there! If anything's happened to it!" He moved on in midsentence, battling the throng to get his own vehicle.

Angelina stood amid all the hustle going on, but feeling strangely as if she were alone. In her shame, she was certain that was true: she was alone now. Even in the humid night, she shivered and hugged her arms about her. How cold she was, as if she had been flung into a damp cell where light never entered.

David blamed her. Something terrible has happened to the diamond and David has levied the guilt on her.

A Gypsy was always suspect. Once a Gypsy, forever a Gypsy. It was a brand on the soul that no amount of fame or fortune could erase. And, oh...her soul was on fire, burning, burning! A billion oceans of tears could never douse the flames licking at her heart.

Chapter Eighteen

Out of some perverse sense of futility, Angelina decided to see the farce to its final conclusion. It took a few moments, but she got a cab and twenty minutes later was delivered to the location of the exhibition. There were reporters and police surrounding the building's exterior. It was due to the reporters that she was eventually granted permission to enter. Rushing at her to get statements, they inadvertently confirmed her relationship with David.

"He wants me with him," Angelina insisted to the officer in charge. When he showed a moment's weakness, she took her chance and pushed on by. Before she could be apprehended, she had swept past the other posted officials and all the way to the entrance of the Phoenix Room.

At the threshold of the room she was finally halted by an armed guard, but through the open door she could easily observe the drama unfolding within. The fact that its star was none other than Ramon made her hold her breath rather than call out to David. She supposed she should not have been surprised, yet even so, the scene before her was as pathetic as it was inevitable. Ramon had finally made the big time; unfortunately, not in the way he had anticipated.

Her brother was standing by himself near the center of the room, only three feet from the podium that had once held the Phoenix Diamond. He appeared to be as baffled by its disappearance as the police who surrounded him. Again and again, he repeated the litany of "I don't know where it's gone!"

No one believed him.

Strangely, even after everything he had done against her, her heart went out to him. Angelina knew him well, and for once he was telling the truth. Her mind flashed back over the years, and she saw him in quick successive flashes: now a boy, then as an older teenager, a young man, and as he was now before her. In each and every stage of his life he had tried for something better. He had the right motivation, but confused by desperation and fueled by pride, he had chosen all the wrong methods of elevating himself.

"I swear to you! It was missing when I arrived. Bloody hell!" he raged on. "What do you think, I'm magic? I can make a diamond as big as a goose egg disappear into the air? All of this for nothing!"

Then, seeing Angelina in the doorway, he suddenly pointed his finger, shouting, "It's all your fault!"

David also turned. Seemingly perplexed, he held her in his vision for a moment, then looked back at Ramon. "Why? Why is this her fault?"

Angelina's heart stopped. All movement, every sound in the room seemed, likewise, to freeze. David waited. Angelina waited. The sentence was about to be pronounced.

"Because," Ramon fumed, glaring at her from his place of inquisition, "she wouldn't help me. And now, do you see the joke? Someone else has got the stone anyway, Angelina. All your stupid nobility was for nothing."

Not guilty!

It was as if the world had suddenly gone from black and white into blazing technicolor. The film again speeded up. Sounds were normal. Angelina began to breathe again.

"She wouldn't help you?" David repeated.

"No," Ramon said. "She refused. She was too bloody good, or something, to involve herself. Maybe it was that. Or maybe..." And then Ramon did an extraordinary thing, something uncharacteristic, upon which Angelina reflected again and again in the weeks that followed.

It was as if, when he looked at her, he suddenly saw her through clear eyes, through eyes unclouded by personal motive or greed or fear. There was a softening of Ramon's expression, and a long hesitation. Maybe he, too, was taking a quick backward trip through time, seeing her as the child she had been, then as the teenage girl, and on through the pages of a mental family scrapbook.

For a moment she felt as if she and Ramon were together against the whole world, a different species apart from those other humans surrounding them. As they had been since birth, she and he were creatures bent on survival in an inhospitable planet. They had only each other. They were family. They were Gypsies. There was that bond.

Finally Ramon drew his eyes away from her. In a different voice, he said, "Maybe it was because she loved you…maybe that's why she was too stupid to help her brother."

It was his apology to her. It was his way of holding out his hand and trying, even at this latest of dates, at this last hour, to help put things right between them again; or, more correctly, at last.

Angelina saw the tears in Ramon's eyes, not of sorrow really, or of fear, but strangely they seemed to be born of some inner realization, a knowledge come too late perhaps—but welcome just the same.

Angelina nodded, and Ramon smiled faintly, their silent pact acknowledged.

Ramon looked back to David and the police inspectors. To Angelina, her brother appeared like an actor who had gone offstage for a scene and was now back, sure of his lines, reveling in the chance to take over the audience once again. The familiar cockiness was back in his voice when he said, "You know, you don't really have a thing on me. Breaking and entering. Intent. But I didn't get the stone, so what can you say about that?" He smirked triumphantly.

"Maybe five years," returned one of the police.

"Five minutes!" Ramon scoffed. "That's the time it will take me to beat any system you've got."

To David, Ramon had one more thing to say before being led away under restraint. "She's a lot of trouble, you know? A traitor, too. She's never, never going to be accepted by her people after this. Nothing but a defector. I just hope you know the kind of woman you're dealing with here. Take heed," he said, raising a brow melodramatically. "And," he shouted to Angelina as he was coaxed along by his captors, "you'll never be trusted by any Gypsy so long as you may live!"

But he was kind of laughing as he said it, and seeing him that way, so buoyant, so typically incorrigible, made Angelina break into her own lopsided grin.

The room seemed suddenly darker and colder with Ramon gone, as if a bright light had been extinguished. The curtain was down. She realized it was time for her own exit.

In the briefest of intervals between the time that David could free himself in one sentence from the police, Angelina had disappeared.

David ran after her, but made it too late. From the curb, he saw her leaving in a cab. Quickly, he jumped into his limousine.

His driver lost her twice in traffic, but by the neighborhood, David assumed correctly that she would be going to her father's antique store. He was right, but again arrived too late to apprehend her. There had been a red light, and then a minor mishap. By the time his car came around the block, she was just exiting the darkened shop.

The taxi, with Angelina in it, sped off once again.

It didn't take long to realize that she was on her way back to their apartment; probably, he thought with apprehension, to pack and get the hell away from him for good this time. Suddenly nothing—not even the diamond—seemed as important to him as getting Angelina back into his arms.

She was out of the taxi, going to the door when he leaped from the limousine, calling after her. "Angelina!"

But she appeared not to hear. Or, more likely, she didn't want to speak to him. Twisting the key in the door, she entered the darkened hallway.

Quick as she was, he expected her to be up the stairs and halfway packed by the time he made it into the foyer.

He was therefore surprised when, coming after her, he discovered she hadn't moved from just inside the door. Her attention was directed above them, to the sound of music and a faint thumping noise.

Slowly, she moved forward.

"No—Angelina, no," David said in a hushed voice. He held her back. "I'll call the police."

"There's no need," she said and shook his hand free. Before he could catch hold of her, she was running up the stairs.

David took two steps for every one of hers, but she was still faster. He recalled the first time he had met her in the deli. If anyone needed protection from what waited at the top of the stairs, it was probably going to be him.

As it happened, the second floor sitting room held a mystifying and extraordinary sight. Or was it, David reconsidered as he entered the room after Angelina, an event he was witnessing?

Lights were ablaze and music poured from the radio. Humming along to the tune as he danced solo—arms akimbo, legs kicking, knees dipping—was an aging man. His movements were spritely, his attire lavishly gaudy. He appeared to be a one man festival of bad taste. From one ear dangled a gold hoop. A bandanna covered his graying head, and around his neck dangled a jeweler's supply of gold chains that swung counterpoint to his dance movements. All of this, and a bright red ruffled shirt.

"Father!"

The man did not miss a beat. "Greetings! Greetings and salutations!" With a wink at David, he said, "I am none other than the famous—ah, the infamous— scoundrel, Zoltan!" He twirled around like a dervish and ended up on one knee, arms outstretched. He was panting and David was for a moment worried he might collapse.

"David . . ." Angelina said flatly, "my father."

"Glad you could drop by," David said.

"Thank you," Zoltan returned, grinning. "Oh, while I think of it, I'm afraid one of your windows will need a new lock."

"Speaking of locks, Father—where . . . is . . . it?"

And suddenly there was a flash of brilliant light flying from Zoltan's hand straight into the air.

For a second David could only gape. "It was you?"

"Why not me?" Zoltan did a quick, mock bow and, twirling around on his heel, caught the diamond and proceeded to continue his showy strut in time to the music. With each downbeat, the diamond was sent heavenward until, exasperated, Angelina silenced the radio.

"I knew it!" Angelina raged. "You just couldn't re- sist, could you?"

"Rather crafty of me, wasn't it?" Zoltan said with obvious pride. He threw the diamond to David, who caught it—just barely. "Oh, and don't bother calling the police," he advised with sincerity. "They'll never hold me."

"But, why?" David asked, knowing he was experi- encing all the wrong emotions. He should have been frothing with anger. The most he could muster in the way of emotion was intense curiosity. "All this trouble . . . the danger . . . just to give it back?"

"Oh, it wasn't the diamond's worth," Angelina said with dry fury. "It had nothing to do with the diamond's intrinsic value."

Zoltan nodded. "It wasn't the diamond."

"It was his pride," Angelina explained, giving her father the darkest look David had ever seen her deliver. "It was the challenge. If you'd locked up Mount Everest, he would have tried slipping that in his pocket, as well."

"She brought me the plans, you see—to uncover any holes. It was a good thought, meant to save you from the criminal element," Zoltan said, laughing. "But they weren't genuine, were they? Ha! Good show on your part. But not good enough. It stimulated my sense of adventure, brought the old lust for excitement to the fore again." He sighed, as if mentally savoring earlier exploits when such exhilaration was the common order of the day. "I used my own imagination to devise the most clever security system possible, and then I used my imagination to defeat it."

"My father was once the best," Angelina commented with grudging respect. "Putting it another way, you might say he doesn't take well to retirement."

"I am still the best," Zoltan inserted quickly. "Am I not?" he asked, seeking confirmation from David. "There, man, you've the proof in your hand. Anyway, when you report this to the police—which I'm sure you must—make certain to spell the name right. That damned Antonio! Some good press for me will cook his goose but good, hey, Angelina?"

Angelina shook her head, too furious to speak. Then, suddenly, she ran to him. Sobbing, she threw herself into Zoltan's arms, burying her head against his chest as she had a hundred times during her childhood. "Why?" she demanded, the word a long cry of pain. "Why did you ruin it all? I wanted you to have your dream. And you came so close, so close..."

"Well, now, now," Zoltan crooned, patting her back. He looked to David then, as if he needed the other man to support him in the coming lie. "I've a new idea. This one will make me a fortune. So you needn't worry, little one."

"I do worry...I do..." Angelina sobbed.

"Take care of my daughter for me," he said to David. His voice almost broke. "She's too soft for a Gypsy. Nothing but a liability."

"Liabilities are my speciality," David said quietly. "A hobby of mine."

Zoltan nodded. "I know. I know." He tried to free himself from Angelina, but she clung tightly to him.

"No...no..." she said, "You're not leaving."

But Zoltan pushed her gently away.

"Don't go," she said. "You can stay. We'll make it all okay again. The store, everything...it will all work this time, Father. Please...please...just once more."

As he backed toward the door, he said, "I am a Gypsy, Angelina. It is what I am. I follow the wind."

"And I'm your daughter!"

"No, you—" his voice broke even as the single tear dropped down his cheek "—you are Angelina—your own self. Whatever, whoever you want to be. And you follow the stars."

He was half out the door when he turned back and said, as if in afterthought, "The star...the right star to follow . . . that one's always in here." He made a quick jabbing motion to his heart. "Inside. Then there's never a wrong turn."

And then he was gone.

For a long while Angelina did not take her eyes from the door, trying to memorize the image of her father. "It's the last time," she said quietly. "I'll never see him again."

"You don't know that," David said, and came to her.

But she did know it, and so did Zoltan. "That was my goodbye."

Tentatively, David put his arms around her. She did not resist, nor did she encourage any further intimacy. The wounds he had inflicted were still raw.

The room was very quiet, and suddenly David also sensed that Zoltan had paid them his last visit. He did not know how he knew, only that he knew, as if that knowledge had been transferred to him from Angelina's heart to his. And perhaps, he thought, that was the true secret of the Gypsies' strange powers. With hearts open to life, feelings traveled unobstructed.

Angelina finally turned to him.

Before she could form the words, David placed his finger upon her lips. "I know," he said. "It hurt tonight. I hurt you. It's going to take time. I'll wait. For as long as it takes," he said gently, "even if it means forever."

Her dark eyes were wide. "How did you know that's what I was just going to say?"

David only smiled.

How strange it all was, this crazy life, Angelina thought as she kicked leaves along a Paris sidewalk. On the third week of October, the world was dressed in scarlet, with accessories of glowing amber. A saucy, frisky month! A Gypsy of a month, she thought. A smile ignited her face, just as a somber-looking man passed by her. He caught the merriment, and for a moment, off his guard of seriousness, a light of joy flickered briefly behind the gray, sad eyes. Then he remembered and returned to his job of worrying, slogging heavily along.

Life, itself, seemed to move so slowly as one lived it day by day. But in one year lives were turned upside down and around and back up again. In evidence, she offered her own life.

It had taken a while to heal, but David had helped by allowing it all to happen naturally. How amazing the heart was! So courageous! What a tough little organ it was. In any battle of the spirit, its very softness vanquished personalities composed of the hardest tempered steel.

Their marriage was to be in one more week. It was going to be a Forever Marriage. She knew this . . . and so did David, whose instincts seemed peculiarly sharpened of late. She had teased him that he was becoming a Gypsy! And, instead of grumbling, he had smiled and hugged her, as if it were a compliment.

Perhaps the greatest gift David could have given her was his total acceptance of her—past and present. He even insisted on paying for legal counsel for Ramon. When he suggested it, Angelina was shocked. "You'd do that? He almost ruined you!"

"But Ramon's family!" Beneath his breath, he did add, "Devil that he is."

On the day of the trial, she and David arrived to lend Ramon emotional support. However their presence

proved unnecessary. Ramon, it turned out, had somehow slipped out of custody that morning.

Again, David only laughed when reporters were there
to snap his picture in association with the aborted trial.
He did not care what the world thought, nor what his
family thought. One did not live his life for others, but
for one's own self, he said. He cited Zoltan as the source
of his philosophy.

In spite of what on the surface appeared to be another crisis caused by Ramon, she and David were both
in good spirits as they drove home that day. Upon entering the town house they were even joking. But simultaneously and instantaneously, their laughter faded.

"Oh, no..." David said, drawing Angelina back toward the front door.

"There's someone here," Angelina said, also sensing a change in the environment.

"And this time I don't hear any music."

Angelina was half frightened and half impressed.
David was amazing. Then Angelina saw the muddy heel
mark and realized David's powers of divination were
not all that refined. "Fraud!" she said.

"Shh, Angelina..."

"David...they've gone. Whoever it was came and
left." As proof, she pointed out another footprint,
headed in the opposite direction.

"Quite right, Watson."

Together they inventoried the house for missing
items. Mysteriously, nothing appeared touched. And
then, in the bedroom, the puzzle was solved. Placed in
the center of the bed was a large box wrapped in white
and silver wedding paper. In it was a magnificent glass
sculpture of a butterfly with its wings unfurled. Below,

also executed in glass, was the empty cocoon from which the butterfly had escaped.

Angelina opened the accompanying card. "To my sister, with love. May I someday also become what I am not yet."

Touched as she was, Angelina's natural conclusion was that Ramon had swiped the gift.

David insisted otherwise. "You ought to have a little faith," he said.

"I'm going to hit you on the head with this!" Angelina returned. "I know my brother."

"I thought I knew you once. I was wrong."

Nevertheless she insisted on proving her point, and with David carrying the alleged purloined gift, marched back to the store whose name was written on the box.

"Excuse me," she said to the clerk, "but well . . . this is rather embarrassing, but perhaps this might have flown out of your store on its own?"

The manager was promptly called. "Oh," he said, "you've come, have you? Yes, yes . . . I'll just be a moment." He returned almost immediately with another, smaller box. "The gentleman who purchased this asked that you be especially careful in its handling. He said it's particularly fragile. And of course, very valuable."

David unwrapped the box, and Angelina lifted the tiny crystal butterfly out. The note read, "To all our new beginnings . . ."

Silhouette Special Edition

JUNE TITLES

THE EXECUTIVES
Monica Barrie

ROSE IN BLOOM
Andrea Edwards

FOR NOW, FOREVER
Nora Roberts

SHADOW ON THE SUN
Maggi Charles

GOLDEN FIRESTORM
Anne Lacey

OBJECT OF DESIRE
Jennifer West

Silhouette Special Edition

Available in June

Nora Roberts's sensational

MacGregor Series

Coinciding with the publication of FOR NOW,
FOREVER, the final book in Nora Roberts's
exciting and heart-warming saga of the MacGregor
family, Silhouette Books are re-issuing the original
four novels in Special Collectors' Editions.
Be sure not to miss these super stories, which follow
the lives and loves of the MacGregor children.
Look for PLAYING THE ODDS, TEMPTING
FATE, ALL THE POSSIBILITIES and ONE
MAN'S ART.

Silhouette Special Edition

JULY TITLES

HONORABLE INTENTIONS
Kate Meriwether

DANGER IN HIS ARMS
Patti Beckman

THEIR SONG UNENDING
Anna James

RETURN TO EDEN
Jeanne Stephens

**THE SHOWGIRL AND
THE PROFESSOR**
Phyllis Halldorson

FIRE AT DAWN
Linda Shaw